TALES OF AKELDAMA

JOSE NEPTUNO MARTINEZ

Follow me on social media:
Instagram: @neptunoauthor
Facebook.com/neptunoauthor
TikTok: @neptuno.books
www.neptunomartinez.com

Cover design concept: Jose Neptuno Martinez
Book translation: Jose Neptuno Martinez
Original title: *Relatos de Akeldama (2024)*
Published by: Jose Neptuno Martinez
Book design: Jose Neptuno Martinez
First edition

ISBN: 979-8-218-53745-6

With great love and gratitude for her patience, to my wife Yeimy, and to my children, Sebastian and Aidan.

In memory of our beloved Merlin, our furry friend, who left us with a profound lesson in unconditional love.

CONTENTS

"*Then one of the twelve, called Judas Iscariot, went unto the chief priests, and said unto them, what will ye give me, and I will deliver him unto you? And they covenanted with him for thirty pieces of silver. And from that time he sought opportunity to betray him.*"
Matthew 26:14-16 King James Version (KJV)

"*If you are seeking revenge, you'd better dig two graves, for one of them will be your own.*"
Chinese Proverb

SOMETIMES IT'S BETTER TO TURN THE OTHER CHEEK

The bustle of tourists subsided somewhat, especially given the hour. Most of the crowds gathered during the peak morning hours, when everyone seized the opportunity to visit the main tourist attractions of the ancient city. He glanced at his Apple Watch; it was 5:17 PM on Tuesday, August 9th. The afternoon was beautiful, with pleasant weather and a sky bluer than usual. Few clouds floated by. Everything seemed brighter; the shades of the stone blocks of the ancient buildings appeared more vivid, at least that's how he perceived them while strolling through the cobblestone streets. In truth, he was quite enjoying these afternoon walks. His new routine. Something he hoped would become a new habit. In a way, he felt like a tourist.

He found it amusing that despite living there nearly all his life, he had never taken the time to truly explore the city. It

1

was a strange sensation, realizing that even though his body was present, his mind always seemed elsewhere, preoccupied with other things. For several weeks, he'd been feeling good about himself, a first since his retirement almost a year ago. At last, he seemed to have found the peace of mind that had eluded him for so long. He was glad he'd finally followed the advice he'd often ignored: to see a therapist who could help him silence—or at least numb—the demons that haunted him, threatening to destroy him. One in particular.

Who would have told Yaakov Katz that at fifty-five years old, he could start a new life? Who could have imagined he would find a stable partner again, even someone fifteen years younger than him? And beautiful, too. He seemed to have found the path to a new beginning, despite having been convinced it would be impossible to leave his old life behind. But now it seemed possible. Mental peace.

Yaakov reached a pleasant, wide alley that bordered what appeared to be a small park, shaded by Mediterranean pines and cypresses. It was a quiet place; there were some local shops and small restaurants with terraces and round tables set up outside. The presence of people was sparse. Each person in their own world. He bought a bottle of water.

His first choice was coffee, but he wanted to avoid caffeine and anything else that might make him anxious. He settled on a bench next to a tree. In front of him, a pleasant view. In the distance, one could see one of the domes of the Church of the Holy Sepulchre. The ringing of bells could be heard far off. The air whistled between the walls of the ancient buildings, creating a monastic feeling of tranquility. He looked around and observed the people passing by and now accompanying him in his new role as a tourist. He was a keen observer. In his old life, he had to be.

Some children ran and laughed, couples of all ages came and went. Tourists, mostly. Nearby, the chords of an acoustic guitar resonated. A group of young people were singing slightly off-key songs, seemingly not taking it too seriously; they laughed mischievously, it seemed. After all, they were young.

He checked his watch again, and when he felt that everything was fine, that it was safe, he opened the book he had with him. A novel by John Grisham. He enjoyed the legal thriller genre. As he arranged the page where he had left off, he reflected on how beautiful Jerusalem was. An ancient city. Such an overwhelming amount of history concentrated in one place. Impressive. How much of humanity's fate had been written and decided there, but also how many conflicts and endless wars plagued the region. He decided to stop his thoughts abruptly, as the therapist had warned him that it was like throwing coal into the furnace of his personal hell. He decided to focus on the novel. He took a sip of water. He smiled, and before he knew it, he was absorbed in his reading. All worries and tempting memories vanished. The street noises and ambient voices turned into hypnotic murmurs. He stayed like that for quite a while.

He was about to turn the page when a brutal shadow engulfed him, shattering his peace of mind. What a terrible feeling! What was happening? He had rarely felt such confusion, and he had faced all sorts of dangers. The shadow that covered him snuffed out the light entirely, accompanied by a blow that echoed in his right ear. He felt suffocated, short of breath. It all happened in a matter of seconds. Had his end come? Was he dead? Is this what it feels like? Was the world over? What was going on?! Thoughts raced through his mind like a bullet train. He felt the adrenaline flooding his body. His survival instinct kicked in. It took control of his body and made him leap like a frightened feline; his senses began to sharpen, assessing his surroundings.

He thought he heard sinister, mocking laughter fading into murmurs. In desperation, he brought both hands to his head but couldn't find it; in its place was something solid, hard, like a giant helmet. With instinctive swiftness, he tore it off and threw it into the air. The light and fresh air returned, but so did an overwhelming confusion; old demons began to appear. He heard whatever he had removed from his head rolling across the floor. He looked at it: at first glance, it seemed like a crude plastic object, but after examining it, he realized it was a black bucket, the kind used for storing paint or carrying liquids. "What the hell?" he muttered.

He had no idea what was happening. Had someone put a bucket on his head? He looked around, searching for the culprit. At first, everyone seemed suspicious. Some appeared unaware of anything, while others watched him with bewilderment. An old demon in the form of visceral anger made its presence felt. "*Yes, someone put a bucket on your head and hit you,*" it whispered in his ear, prompting Yaakov to chase after an invisible enemy.

He ran around, looking for the assailant. He was in excellent physical condition, allowing him to move with agility. Everyone seemed suspicious to him; he felt they were mocking him. He kept returning to the spot where the attack occurred, thinking the attacker always returns to the scene of the crime. Confusion was now his master. He continued like this for a while until he realized he was making a pathetic fool of himself. He understood what people might be thinking of him: a tall, athletic man despite his age, with rough features on a fine face, acting like a mime chasing imaginary beings. No doubt they thought he was a drug addict or mentally unbalanced.

He felt embarrassed; his inner self gave him a good scolding. "*Why are you acting like this? I don't recognize you at all.*" The old Yaakov would never have behaved this way. He decided to calm down. He took a deep breath. He composed himself and tidied his hair. He picked up the book that was on the floor, along with his water bottle. He drained it in one gulp. He realized he was sweating. He had lost track of time. Everything seemed to return to normal. The young people he had been watching continued to sing off-key to the rhythm of the guitar, and the tourists kept coming and going. Only a couple of people were watching him with bewilderment. One thing was certain: the attack did happen; he hadn't imagined it or gone crazy, as the black bucket lay on the ground. The *smoking gun.* He picked it up, examined it, and left it in a corner. He decided to leave the place.

As he drove back to his apartment, his mind buzzed with the incident. Confusion enveloped him. What was it all about? Was it a warning or a cruel prank from an old enemy? But who, and why? A fire ignited in his gut, visceral anger rising, but he extinguished it with deep breaths, regaining his composure.

When he reached his apartment, Abigail was there, waiting. As he entered, she sensed something was wrong.

Concerned, she took his hand and guided him to the small living room.

"Tell me, what happened?" she asked. Yaakov recounted the terrible experience. Initially, Abigail shared his confusion, but as they discussed it further, she suggested it had all been a bad joke. The method seemed to indicate as much. Like all major tourist cities, Jerusalem is full of idle wanderers with no occupation or apparent purpose. If there had been another motive, perhaps he would be in the hospital now, recovering from a beating, or worse, he might not even be telling the tale. Abigail stood up and went to the kitchen, pouring him a glass of his favorite wine to help him relax.

"It's really nothing, don't overthink it, love. You've come so far with Tamar, your therapist. Don't let this little setback undo all the progress you've made." He nodded, still uncertain.

"What I don't understand is, if it was a prank, why me?"

"It could have been anyone. From what you told me, you were off guard in a public place, the perfect target for a bored prankster," she said gently, cupping his face with a gentle touch.

"You're right. I'm not going to let this destroy my peace and tranquility," he replied, smiling. Abigail looked at him inquisitively and couldn't help but laugh.

"I can just picture you, with a bucket on your head," she said, bringing her hands to her mouth to stifle her laughter. Now she was letting out cute little whimpers. If not for the fact that Yaakov found her beautiful when she doubled over in laughter, with her long black hair, almond skin, and delicate features giving her the air of a mischievous teenager, he might have flown into a rage as in the past. But he was different now. He ended up joining her, laughing at himself.

He had a night from hell. Sleep eluded him. A terrible nightmare woke him, reliving the incident but in a different setting. He was in a place resembling a medieval dungeon. Dim light flickered from torches mounted on stone walls. Yaakov was bound hand and foot to a chair, his head covered with a wooden bucket reeking of rot. The smell was unbearable. He struggled to breathe, thrashing against his restraints. Then, a shadow draped in shrouds removed the bucket. As his blurred vision cleared, a grotesque face loomed before him—a man who looked like a leper, his face oozing pus and worms. The stench was putrid. He mocked Yaakov with derision.

"You're a pathetic fool!" the leper bellowed, turning toward the shadows, draped in tattered rags. Their faces remained hidden, but their grotesque, sinister laughter reverberated in unison. Yaakov stared as the monstrous figure seized another bucket, brimming with something thick and foul. The stench was suffocating. As the creature lurched closer, he discerned the revolting contents—excrement mixed with decaying human remains. His scream tore through the silence as he braced for it to be dumped on his head. Then Yaakov jolted awake, drenched in sweat, gasping for air.

"What's wrong, Yaakov?" Abigail asked, half-asleep.

"Nothing, just a bad dream. Go back to sleep," he replied, trying not to worry her.

He got up for a glass of water and went to the small balcony of the apartment to get some fresh air. He massaged his forehead. He returned to bed but couldn't sleep anymore; he was restless. A train of thoughts sped through his mind. He started feeling anxious, trying to keep his distress from escalating. It wasn't the nightmare that made him feel this way. In his former life, he had been through worse. It was another feeling that tormented him, one that kept him from sleeping and drove him to act the next morning.

Having not slept a wink, he took a shower and got ready early. He didn't want to eat breakfast, just made himself a coffee. Abigail, still curled up in the sheets, asked where he was going so early. Yaakov told her he wanted to take advantage of the morning to run some errands and that the sooner he did them, the better. Still in bed, she bid him goodbye with a kiss and he told her he'd see her later for lunch. As soon as he left his apartment, he took out his cell phone and dialed a number.

"I need to see you in your office, it's urgent." He said nothing more and hung up.

The discreet yet modern two-story building where he was to conduct his business was on the outskirts of the city, in a quiet, rural area that offered privacy and resembled a place of rest. Yaakov drove his black 2022 Kia for about five hundred meters along a narrow road until he reached a guardhouse, where a guard met him. He eyed him cautiously, almost suspiciously. It was a common reaction.

"What's the purpose of your visit?" the guard asked bluntly.

"I'm expected by Senior Officer *Katsa*, Yatom Abramov," Yaakov replied, handing over an unusual identification. Upon seeing it, the guard asked no further questions and let him pass.

He entered the building with familiarity; several people recognized him and greeted him from afar. Upon reaching the reception area, an odd feeling washed over him. For a moment, he wondered what he was doing there. He was about to turn around and leave when a man in his sixties, with graying hair and dressed in an impeccable suit adorned with official insignias, approached him. The man seemed surprised by his presence.

"Yaakov? What brings you here, brother? Don't tell me you've grown tired of retirement already?" he said, raising an eyebrow as he gave him a firm handshake.

"Not at all, Ben," Yaakov replied, shaking his head.

"My days at the agency are over. I just came to visit and catch up with my good friend Yatom," he said, smiling, trying to downplay the matter.

They chatted for a few minutes before Yaakov said goodbye to the man in the suit.

"Don't forget to call me one of these days so we can go for that meal we've been planning," he said to Yaakov.

A young receptionist directed him to Yatom's office. It was a long hallway. As he walked, memories from his old life came flooding back, as if they had happened yesterday. So many experiences, so many memories. It hadn't been easy to decide to retire, but certain circumstances, including his fragile emotional state, had forced his hand. If he'd stayed another year, the ticking time bomb would have exploded with devastating consequences.

Yaakov had spent a little over thirty years as a special agent of the Mossad, Israel's enigmatic intelligence agency, tasked with covert operations, espionage, and counter-terrorism, not only in the region but across much of the world. He was a distinguished agent, participating in missions of great significance, some of which nearly cost him his life.

Due to his experience, he rose to a high-ranking position within the agency's cryptic department of secret information gathering, attaining the rank of *katsa*, which in Hebrew is an acronym for field intelligence officer. However, all this prestige and experience came at a high price. Over the years, his emotional and mental state deteriorated. It cost him a divorce and the loss of several friendships and family relationships. He had always been a man of strong and strict character, but the high level of demands and stress that came with being part of Mossad gradually turned him from a grumpy man into a violent brute. On more than one occasion, he was accused of torture and suspected of murder against criminals and terrorists captured during missions. They could never prove anything against him.

The breaking point came when he nearly beat a fellow agent to death. The incident occurred during a meeting where they were discussing a sensitive issue requiring impactful decisions.

Yaakov proposed a certain course of action, which David Mizrachi, another high-ranking agent, strongly opposed, expressing his disagreement with derision and arrogance. There was already bad blood between them, largely due to David's biting and haughty behavior, who, out of professional jealousy, seemed determined to find opportunities to undermine Yaakov in front of their superiors.

He knew how to push Yaakov's buttons.

"We have this guy here who wants to lecture us on morality and tell us how we should adapt our actions to the recommendations of the human rights commission to avoid interference that might affect the mission's development when he's the first to ignore them. It's like an orangutan trying to teach the zoo trainer how to behave," he said, triggering a burst of laughter from the group.

"By the way, do you know how Yaakov wishes his wife a happy birthday? With a punch in the nose," David continued, as if performing a stand-up routine, laughing shrilly.

That was the spark that lit the fuse. With a swift, unexpected move, driven by adrenaline, Yaakov lunged at his colleague, knocking him down with an elbow that shattered his nose. Once on top of him, in a cruel twist of irony, he became a wild orangutan, delivering punches at a furious, uncontrolled pace to David's face. Yaakov's expression transformed into a mask of terror. His hazel eyes seemed to turn crimson, nearly bulging out of their sockets. If those present hadn't intervened, he would have left David looking like a living portrait of a Picasso, heavily influenced by Stephen King.

David spent a week in intensive care due to the brutal beating. Yaakov was suspended for two weeks. He avoided jail because his lawyer argued that the attack had been provoked by the victim himself, as seen in the security camera footage. He was only ordered to pay a hefty compensation. After that incident, he became somewhat of a recluse. Many of his colleagues treated him with a mix of fear and reverence, trying to avoid him as much as possible. Each day became a torment as he struggled to manage the stress and pressures of the job. He suffered from anxiety and anger attacks. Any minor incident would set him off. All of this contributed to his family breakdown and a chaotic divorce, complete with a restraining order.

Thanks to the intervention of one of his closest friends, Yatom Abramov, a high-ranking officer among the *katsas*, Yaakov was pulled back from the brink and introduced to an excellent therapist: Tamar Friedman, who specialized in intermittent explosive disorders, the clinical diagnosis given to Yaakov. Over the years, the two of them had formed a deep friendship, solidified by countless shared experiences. They were the same age and had similar tastes. Yatom became the only person who could calm Yaakov's raging temper, bringing him back to his senses during his crises. He was the one who urged him to break free from what was destroying him.

Mossad granted him early retirement with full benefits, considering not only his diagnosis but also his years of service and contributions to the agency. From that moment on, Yaakov underwent intensive rehabilitation therapy, designed to help him confront his two main demons: anger and vengeance.

When he met Yatom, they greeted each other with a warm and sincere embrace. It had been a couple of months since they'd last spoken.

"You look great, brother," Yatom said. They exchanged a few words about trivial matters to ease into the heart of the conversation. He invited Yaakov to sit. His office was spacious, with a large window offering a panoramic view. In the distance, the ancient city of Jerusalem could be seen. It was like looking at the past through a futuristic viewpoint. The desk was large and made of black glass. As one would expect from a high-level intelligence agent's office, it featured a massive touch screen in the center. On the opposite corner of his desk were a couple of computers and two elongated monitors displaying a series of alphanumeric characters that could easily resemble an alien language. It gave the impression of a sophisticated Wall Street stockbroker's office.

"Tell me, brother, what brings you here? It must be something very important for the great Yaakov to leave his heaven and enter the mouth of hell again," he said with a touch of sarcasm and, more than anything, a sense of intrigue. Yaakov cleared his throat as he rubbed his forehead. He hesitated. It was then that he realized that, despite being an almost childish triviality, if he didn't speak about it, it would become an obsession that wouldn't let him rest.

"Go on," Yatom encouraged him.

"You see, when I finish telling you, you might think I've gone completely insane and that all the therapy sessions were useless. But I'm sure you'll understand my reasons, put yourself in my shoes," he said, shrugging.

"Something so strange happened to me that, for a moment, I began to doubt my own sanity. But even so, I need you to help me prove that I'm not going crazy," he said, looking him straight in the eyes. Yatom looked expectant and, with his expression, urged him to continue.

"Well, here it goes, brother."

Throughout the recounting of events, Yatom's face displayed a range of expressions, from disbelief and confusion to a few laughs he tried hard to stifle, aware of his friend's genuine concern and not wanting to appear as though he were mocking him. When Yaakov finished, Yatom fell silent, crossing his arms and furrowing his brow. He reviewed the details with his analytical mind and concluded, like Abigail, that everything pointed to him being the victim of a cruel prank.

"I agree," Yaakov said. "But why was I chosen? And if it was just a bad joke, why didn't the prankster reveal themselves? Or rather, why couldn't I find them?" he expressed with frustration, a wound to his pride evident in his tone. He couldn't believe that a former Mossad agent had been caught off guard in such a vile and foolish way.

Yatom attempted to downplay the matter, trying to convince him to view it less as a humiliation and more as a comical mishap, invoking the old adage that *even the best poet can get his words tangled.*

"Look, Yatom, I didn't come here just to vent. The real reason is something else," Yaakov stated, his voice serious and abrupt. Yatom sensed it immediately and grew serious.

"I'm going to make a request that might sound insane. I need your support, brother. I want to find out who the bastard

17

was that derailed my peace of mind and fled without facing the consequences. If I don't find out, I won't be at peace, and I don't want it to turn into a sick obsession. I've made significant progress in my therapy, and I don't want something like this to set me back."

"I'll help you. You have my support."

"Thank you, brother."

"Tell me exactly where and when it happened."

The *Sentinel of a Thousand Eyes* was the sophisticated monitoring system with video cameras that Mossad had installed throughout Israel and, of course, in every corner and nook of Jerusalem. Everything and everyone were under surveillance. Privacy invasion was the agency's specialty, a necessary evil in a region constantly in conflict and at risk of terrorist attacks. Much was at stake in the Holy City, where the *devil* is always on the loose. As if asking for a glass of water, Yatom picked up the phone and ordered the footage from the location, date, and time provided by Yaakov.

In less than five minutes, an officer named Elias Biton entered the office. Yaakov recognized him, though during his time with the agency, he had little interaction with Biton, who had joined just a few months before Yaakov left.

The officer greeted him with familiarity and respect. He

was holding a tablet, which, following Yatom's instructions, he linked to a seventy-inch screen installed on one end of the office, in what appeared to be a small lounge area with two long sofas and a glass table in the center. Yatom motioned for them to get comfortable there. They sat down, and the officer operated the tablet. A menu instantly appeared on the screen, with various options similar to what YouTube displays for selecting a video. Yaakov's impatience and nervous anticipation were obvious on his face. He clasped his hands together. Yatom watched him for a moment and then instructed the officer to play the video.

The video showed a wide shot of the alley where Yaakov had arrived. The area was surrounded by small shops and restaurants with terraces. Within the frame, the Church of the Holy Sepulchre and other historic buildings in the area could be seen. Yaakov stood up and walked to the screen to indicate the path he took through the place, pointing to the exact spot where he had sat to read his novel, as he hadn't yet appeared in the video.

"Please, fast forward a bit," he urged Officer Biton. The officer complied, and soon, among the diverse group of people, Yaakov could be seen walking. As if watching a key play in a soccer match, he remained still, expectant. He swallowed hard. He saw himself sit down, take a sip from his water bottle, and focus on his reading. It was then that the devil appeared on the screen.

Just a few meters away from where Yaakov sat absorbed in his book, on a stone bench shaded by several pine trees, there was a small group of three young people, aged between twenty and twenty-five. Two were attractive, blonde women. One wore a short, light floral dress, and the other a fitted tank top and white shorts. The third was a man, sitting between them. He wore a black T-shirt and khaki shorts. His ridiculous haircut resembled that of an Amazonian native. He had black hair, a round face, and pronounced eyebrows. Not very tall. He was somewhat handsome, but his arrogance was obvious from a mile away. They looked every bit like American tourists, as was later confirmed.

The young man was holding an acoustic guitar and appeared to be serenading his two companions, who were giggling and flirting at his off-key notes. While he strummed a few chords on his guitar, he looked intently toward where Yaakov was sitting, cracked a slight smile, revealing his squirrel-like teeth, and glanced at his companions, giving them a signal. They nodded as if they had read his mind. He then signaled to another person, a man with olive skin, wearing a white tank top and black pants, positioned on the other side, almost directly across from Yaakov. This man pretended to be looking at his phone screen but was actually setting up the camera mode to record. He was ready. The three of them shared a conspiratorial grin.

Without stopping his singing, the man with the indigenous haircut stood up from his seat and, from behind where he had been sitting, pulled out a black bucket. Moving silently with surprising agility, he walked over to Yaakov, circling around to stand directly behind him. At that moment, Yatom asked the officer to zoom in to focus on the individuals.

In a swift motion, he placed the bucket over Yaakov's head and, with his right palm, struck it on the side, making a sound like a muted bell. Leaping back like a gazelle, he returned to his place. With great speed, the woman in the short dress handed him the guitar, and, feigning innocence, he continued with his sinister serenade. They tried to mask their vulgar prank with sardonic smiles. It all happened so quickly that no one around noticed, or perhaps they simply didn't care.

Almost simultaneously, Yaakov sprang up like a startled cat, tearing off the bucket as if it were a giant spider. If he had done it just seconds earlier, he would have seen his attacker. His face contorted, his gaze fierce, like a predator searching for its prey. He moved his head in all directions, as if following the beat of a heavy metal song. He began running around the place as if trying to escape the confusion of a disaster. The sinister pranksters made superhuman efforts not to burst out laughing at Yaakov's reaction, who ran around like a headless chicken while the other people looked on with expressions that clearly said, "What's wrong with this crazy guy?"

The accomplice, who was still recording, chose to put away his phone and discreetly enter the café on the corner, as Yaakov passed by him and gave him a murderous look but kept moving. The video continued until the part where Yaakov regained his composure and walked away from the scene. Officer Biton was about to pause it, but Yaakov stopped him; he wanted to keep watching the final scene.

When the three young men saw that the danger was gone, they burst into convulsive laughter, almost hysterical, like maniacs. Nasal, discordant howls filled the air. The man in the tank top approached and joined the group of clowns, who were celebrating their prank with tears streaming down their faces.

Yaakov was glued to the screen. His blank stare made him look like a mannequin. Yatom and the officer exchanged glances.

"Yaakov, are you alright?" Yatom asked. Yaakov seemed to snap out of his trance. He shook his head slightly and put his hand on his forehead, remaining serious.

"Well, what are your thoughts? Do you think this will help

you feel at ease now?" Yatom inquired, raising his eyebrows with genuine interest.

"I suppose," Yaakov replied, shrugging. His expression was vacant, unlike Yatom and Officer Biton, who were pressing their lips together as their cheeks began to flush. Yaakov noticed them.

"What the hell can you do? I guess I got to play the fool for fate this time," he said with a resigned gesture.

Like pressure cookers, the Mossad agents exploded with laughter. Officer Biton tried to stifle his laughter, lowering his face and covering his mouth with his hand. Yatom struggled to contain himself, convulsing with laughter. For a few moments, Yaakov watched them in disbelief until he finally let out a loud laugh, which, unlike the others, was devoid of joy.

"Forgive me, brother. I couldn't help it. Don't take it the wrong way or as mockery, but what happened to you is absurdly ridiculous. The act itself is what's funny," Yatom explained, hiding the true reason for his amusement, which was seeing his former colleague, a distinguished and irate intelligence officer who had escaped all kinds of dangers, now the victim of a stupid prank, running like a madman with a bucket on his head.

He was making a tremendous effort not to burst into another fit of laughter.

"It sure was funny, huh?" Yaakov replied, watching Officer Biton, who, grinning from ear to ear, was trying to distract himself by fiddling with the tablet. Yaakov let out a forced laugh and put his hand on Yatom's shoulder, trying to pretend that everything now seemed like a silly twist of fate to be taken lightly. That was when the secretary interrupted them to inform Yatom of an important call on his main phone.

"Excuse me for a moment, I have to take this," he apologized.

Yaakov, still laughing and taking advantage of his old colleague being occupied, casually, as if it were a trivial conversation, questioned Officer Biton about the technical capabilities of the surveillance technology Mossad was currently using.

"How advanced is the algorithm and database for facial recognition? Have they been upgraded? Or are we still relying on our friends at the FBI?" he questioned in a challenging tone. Biton smiled, taking the bait.

"Want a demonstration?" he replied with a smug attitude.

"Right now, I'll give you a little demonstration of our prowess. Here you go, every detail of those who played the prank on you." Yaakov feigned disbelief, squinting his eyes.

The officer manipulated his tablet, reopened the video file, and zoomed in on the face of the guitarist with indigenous hair. He clicked on him, and immediately, alphanumeric characters appeared at the top of the screen. A few seconds later, a box opened, displaying a series of additional data and photographs that Officer Biton reviewed on a new tab.

"Here he is," he said triumphantly.

"The prankster's name is Justin Richards, twenty-three years old, from Riverside, California. He's a programming student at the University of California and, well—" he paused, "what do we have here? Our friend turns out to be quite a celebrity. He has a YouTube channel with over five million subscribers and, as you might imagine, he makes viral videos of all kinds of pranks and extravagant challenges. His channel is called *Mr. Justin Hacks*. He has the luxury of traveling around the world, as he's making a fortune with his videos."

Upon hearing this, Yaakov's face lit up, and he felt his chest warm. "*So now it's my turn to be the next viral sensation for this big son of a bitch?*" he thought to himself. Biton guessed his reaction.

"Don't worry, I don't think they'll publish the video without your authorization. Being such a big and famous channel, they've been forced to obtain legal consent from the party involved in each prank or challenge. According to the report, in the past, they've faced a couple of hefty lawsuits for publishing without authorization. It's obvious they didn't ask for your consent. They were most certainly scared by your reaction," he smiled.

Yaakov seemed to calm down. It sounded logical.

"The other three people with him are part of his team. The woman in the short dress is named Delia Johnson, she's twenty-two years old and from Palm Beach, California. She is Justin's girlfriend. The other woman is Susan Alva, twenty-three years old, from Mesa, Arizona. The guy who was filming the video is Tim Araya, from Dallas, Texas. He's the oldest at twenty-six."

He continued manipulating his tablet, and photos of the influencers, as well as entry records to the country and their respective passports, began to appear. The validity of the visa they were granted was for one week, from August fourth to the eleventh, 2022. Tomorrow, they were bound to return to Los Angeles on the 10:30 a.m. American Airlines flight.

"They're staying at the *David Citadel Hotel*, and if you want to know what they had for breakfast, I can tell you that too," he said smugly.

"Impressed?"

"Quite."

Yaakov felt relieved, as if he were a prisoner released from a small, claustrophobic stone cell. He got what he was looking for. Maybe now he could rest, or so he fleetingly thought.

"Sorry if I took longer than expected," Yatom remarked upon returning.

"You know how it is, dear Yaakov. Don't tell me you're still watching the video?"

"No, once was enough for me. I'm not a masochist," Yaakov replied, smiling.

"Our good friend here was showing me the technical capabilities of the *Sentinel of a Thousand Eyes*. Impressive. The power to see and know everything at your fingertips. I remember when, in our day, we had to stand for hours in front of what we considered sophisticated computer equipment to carry out intelligence work that can now be done in seconds."

"And you haven't even seen our latest gadgets. But that's, my dear Yaakov, a state secret," he glanced at Officer Biton, and they both smiled.

"Well, gentlemen, I won't take up any more of your time. I've already distracted Israel's sophisticated espionage apparatus from tasks of real importance. I even feel somewhat embarrassed."

"I'll walk you to the door, brother," Yatom said.

Yaakov bid Officer Biton farewell with gratitude, giving him a firm handshake. As they walked down the hall, Yatom displayed genuine concern for his old colleague. He wanted to know if what he saw in the video eased his worries or merely heightened his anxiety.

"I didn't want to tell you, brother, but when you arrived, you seemed unsettled, nervous. I thought you were dealing with something more difficult. Of course, I'm not downplaying the discomfort and frustration that nasty prank caused you," he said, taking him by the arm.

"Don't worry, I feel much calmer now. I must confess that I was very upset because I feared it might be a warning or threat against me or my family for some unresolved debt from the past. More than one person wants to settle the score. But seeing that it was just a prank by some senseless *cryogenic teenagers*, it's like a great weight has been lifted off my shoulders. I just needed to know what the hell happened, to get rid of that uncertainty, and you, my great friend, have helped me in ways you can't imagine. I owe you one," he expressed, pressing his lips and patting Yatom on the shoulder. Yatom felt relieved.

"You know that's what I'm here for, brother, anytime and anywhere."

They said their goodbyes with a strong hug, agreeing to call each other over the weekend to go out with their respective partners for a meal. It was a plan they had talked about for a long time. As he walked towards the parking lot, Yaakov checked his watch. It was 1:27 PM on Wednesday, August tenth. The sky was beginning to cloud over, yet it still felt warm.

He got into his vehicle and sat there, lost in thought. He replayed the incident he had witnessed through the lens of the video, now etched in his mind. He smiled, then suddenly began to angrily pound on the steering wheel, which nearly bent under his blows. He cursed, his jaw clenched like steel, eyes aflame, the very image of a rabid dog.

Taking a deep breath, he struggled to calm down, applying several exercises his therapist had taught him. He was fighting a brutal internal battle with the demon of anger that threatened to emerge from the cavernous hole where it dwelled. He dealt it a stoic blow, forcing it to retreat back to its hiding place.

"I can't let this ruin me," he muttered to himself.

He cleared his mind, took another deep breath, and started his Kia. He drove away.

When he got to his apartment, Abigail wasn't there. He dialed her cell phone.

"I'm going to have a pretty busy afternoon, love. We're on our way to lunch with some important clients, and then we have a project presentation with several investors. You know how it is," she explained.

Abigail was a successful real estate agent, rapidly climbing the ranks in her field. Her tenacity and professionalism were some of the qualities he admired most about her.

"Do you mind eating alone?"

"Don't worry, I'm not very hungry anyway. I just want to rest a bit," he said, with a hint of sadness. She noticed.

"Are you okay? Did you have any trouble with your errands?"

"Well, sort of. You know how sometimes you run into bureaucrats who just ruin your day. Nothing to worry about. We'll talk tonight."

Yaakov threw himself onto a couch and tried to read a book, but it was impossible; he couldn't focus. He decided to settle at his desk. An impulse led him to open his laptop and go to YouTube. He scolded himself for doing so. The curiosity was becoming unbearable. He justified it to himself like a drunk who says, *"Just one more, and then we'll leave."* Part of closing the circle.

He typed *"Mr. Justin Hacks"* into the search bar, pondering for a moment before clicking on the magnifying glass icon.

The main page loaded. The YouTuber's logo was styled with modern letters and flashy colors. A photograph of Justin appeared, showcasing his big, dumb grin. Apparently, his

Amazonian aboriginal hairstyle was part of his personal brand. Yaakov felt a pang in his stomach. He browsed through the entire page, which was plastered with hundreds of videos. The counter showed more than seven hundred uploaded to the platform. Officer Biton had been wrong about something; the total subscriber count was close to reaching six million. It seemed the infamous influencer's fame was skyrocketing.

He navigated to the section of the most recent videos. He felt relieved to see that the video where he had been the main clown wasn't posted yet. *Not yet.* He observed the titles of the most viewed videos: *"You Won't Believe This Old Lady's Reaction When Mistaken for a Movie Star," "The Cake Prank with Chilies Disguised as Delicious Cherries," "I Pretended to Be a Jilted Lover and You Won't Believe Her Reaction," "Find Out Which Countries Have the Best Reactions to Practical Jokes," "How Shopping Turns into Your Worst Nightmare."* That last title caught his attention, and he clicked on it.

In the video, Justin and his team were shown playing pranks on customers in department stores and supermarkets across various cities in the United States. A poor man who was walking through the mattress section of a department store was surprised from behind while crouching to look at the prices. They threw a giant, heavy teddy bear on top of him. The man fell to the ground, disoriented and not knowing what had happened. Instinctively, he desperately fought with the enormous furry mass. The mischief in this case was committed by Tim, who nonchalantly pretended nothing had happened, lying on one of the mattresses as if he were just another customer.

In another segment of the video, a scene set in the book section of a store showed a young man, who resembled a caricature of a bookworm, leafing through titles. His hollow cheeks accentuated the oversized, antiquated glasses awkwardly perched on his nose. Shortly, Delia, Justin's girlfriend, appeared on the scene, provocatively dressed in tight gym attire that left little to the imagination regarding her physical attributes. She was shown flirting with him with sensual insinuations, getting closer to his face, until finally whispering some words in his ear. One didn't have to be a mind reader to know that the poor guy had never been so close to a woman like her. He was ecstatic, completely disarmed by the charms of this seductive she-devil.

The fleeting love charm was shattered when, without prior warning, Justin appeared on the scene, dressed like a mafioso from *The Sopranos*, making a big scene and shouting like an orangutan.

"So, this is the son of a bitch you're sleeping with? Huh?" he howled in a pathetic imitation of *The Godfather's* accent.

Delia pretended to confess to the adultery, at which the introverted geek reacted with extreme nervousness.

"It's not true, it's not true! I don't even know her!" he whimpered with a broken, frantic voice. Delia hugged him.

"It's time to confess our love and stand up to this jerk. You promised me."

"Oh yeah? Well, this is where it ends for you, pig!" said Justin as he pulled out a gun. The man's face showed an expression of sheer terror, and with a scream, he pushed Delia away, ran, and crashed into a shelf of books. Delia and Justin laughed like maniacs.

Yaakov brought his fingers to the bridge of his nose and shook his head. He was about to close the video when another scene appeared, showing a gray-haired man in his fifties, looking like a member of a biker gang, with a surly face. He was intently looking at some items in a wide aisle of what seemed to be a home improvement store. That's when Justin and Tim appeared on the scene.

The first one stayed at the corner of the aisle holding a dolly with a big cardboard box, while Tim approached and stood beside him to distract the man and allow Justin to take action. The man was positioned on the right side of the aisle, while Justin, with great stealth, moved up on the left side with the dolly and the box. He ended up right behind the gray-haired man.

That's when Tim intentionally dropped a tool on the floor, causing the man to turn at the noise. Taking advantage of the distraction, Justin took the huge empty box and, with momentum, threw it over the man, but he wasn't successful, because, thanks to quick reflexes, the man prevented the box from covering him halfway, which was the real intention. He stopped it and, grabbing it with his hands, tore it in two. He immediately turned to where Justin was standing. It didn't take a genius to figure out who the attacker was.

The man raised his guard as if he were a boxer and took an attack position to throw the first punch at Justin's face, who, upon realizing the danger, began emitting some detestable whimpers and bawls like a cartoonish version of a giant baby.

"I want my mommy, wah, wah! Where's my mom, wah, wah?" he said in a nasal voice, contorting his face in an exaggerated manner, pretending to have a mental disability, which clashed with the way he puffed his corn-cob teeth and an awful haircut, managing to confuse the man, who didn't know how to react, the prudence prevailing in him to not make things worse by hitting a mentally impaired person. Confused and flustered, he kicked the cardboard box and left, uttering all kinds of curses.

When the guy was far enough away, Justin and Tim

dropped to the floor, rolling with laughter as if trying to shake off a swarm of wasps.

Yaakov saw himself reflected in the gray-haired man and immediately turned off the video. His vision blurred as an intense heat surged through his body. He felt like he couldn't breathe at times. Clenching his fists, he made one last attempt to contain the inner demon that was triumphantly emerging from the confinement it had endured for so long. It was *Belial*, the great corrupter. He had returned. *"Did you think you could get rid of me?"* the demon sneered. *"What do you gain by resisting?"*

He grabbed the laptop and smashed it against the floor. With a swift movement, he knocked the table over, leaving it upside down in a corner. He picked up a vase and, like a professional pitcher, hurled it against the wall. He would no longer hide his true feelings. To hell with the nonsense Tamar, his therapist, was telling him.

"Why should a man repress his emotions? Who the hell was she to force him to suppress his true feelings? By what right? Why should he treat the incident as an innocent joke and brush it off as if a fly had just landed on him?"

He finally acknowledged openly that he had never felt so humiliated in his life. No one had managed to degrade him and drag his dignity through the sewers like that wretch, *Mr. Justin Hacks,* and his team of disgusting rats.

"How could a Mossad agent of my rank, with so many years of training and experience, who served his country with great honor and decorum, a conqueror of insurmountable obstacles for any mortal, be taken by surprise and turned into a common buffoon of a medieval village? They ridiculed me in front of my Mossad comrades. What would Yatom think of me now?"

A stinging image of Yatom flashed in his mind, standing in a huge, crowded boardroom with the most elite agents of Mossad, ordering Officer Biton to run the most hilarious viral video of recent times.

"Observe our former comrade in arms, *katsa* Yaakov, running like an idiot with a bucket on his head." He could hear the thunderous laughter erupt in the room. He could see each face, with veins bulging on foreheads and faces crimson, choking with laughter.

He ran his hands through his hair, pacing from side to side, engulfed in a sea of lament.

"No, this can't be!" he shouted, his voice breaking.

"What a brutal humiliation!" he cried, tears welling up in his eyes.

An injurious scene of his beloved Abigail came to mind, at a restaurant where the topic to entertain the evening with her most important clients would be the embarrassing scene performed by her partner.

"Guess what happened to my boyfriend yesterday?" Laughter. Yaakov clenched his jaw. He felt dizzy, the horrible sensation of the bucket on his head returning. He began to flail like a madman, trying to get it off. The confusion that engulfed him was so overwhelming that his mind started playing tricks on him.

He seemed to hear an evil laugh behind him. When he turned around, he found himself face to face with Justin's detestable face, his hideous haircut and offensive smile mocking him with the nasally voice he had seen in the video. He threw a strong punch into the air that ended up landing on a brick wall. The adrenaline coursing through his body was so intense that he didn't even feel the cut on his knuckle, which was now bleeding.

"*What am I doing?*" he berated himself, bringing both hands to his face and hanging his head. He stayed like that for a few moments, slowly regaining his composure. Fragments of emotional intelligence began to surface. He stood up and lay down on the couch, taking a deep breath.

"*I can't let this ruin my life. No way. I'm better than this,*" he told himself with determination, nodding.

"But this… this can't just end like this…"

He made a decision. He would pay the prankster leader back in kind. Swift action was of vital importance since time was limited. According to the information provided by Agent Biton, the killers of his emotional stability would leave the country the next day on the 10:30 a.m. flight. As the first step to carry out his plan, he needed to organize his mind and thoughts, as he had to act with precision, speed, and stealth. Maximum concentration; he couldn't afford any mistakes. "I must act like in my best times, like the great *katsa*, and Mossad agent that I was and... still am," he said aloud.

The first task was to clean up the mess in the apartment. He put the table back in its place, picked up the shards of the vase, and hid the broken laptop lying on the floor. He felt a sting in his fist and quickly patched it up, just as he had been taught. He washed his face with cold water, changed his clothes, and dressed in black, including a cap. He put on black work boots, then went to the closet in his room.

Pushing aside the hanging shirts, he revealed a wall with a strange texture. He placed his hand on it and, as if by magic, removed a wooden cover, exposing a safe with a digital combination. He opened it and took out some things, including a black backpack and a compact Walther P99 semi-automatic pistol. He grabbed two cell phones: one that looked like an iPhone and the other an old BlackBerry. He checked that they were charged, as they always should be. He looked at his watch. It was 5:48 p.m. He was already late.

Everything was in order, as if nothing had happened. Luckily, Abigail wasn't very observant; she wouldn't notice the absence of a vase or that the laptop wasn't on the table. If possible, he would go to the store to buy another one. Before leaving the apartment, he made three calls from each of his phones.

The first was brief, to the *David Citadel Hotel*. The second was to ask for a couple of personal favors in exchange for an old debt, as he mentioned to his interlocutor. The third call was to Abigail, to whom he said he was going out to dinner with a couple of old friends who were visiting the city. He hadn't seen them in years, and since they would have a lot to catch up on, it was better not to wait for him for dinner. He hoped not to be late.

It was the last day in the city. The YouTubers received a last-minute invitation to attend the prestigious *Darkthrone* nightclub, one of the most exclusive and modern venues in Jerusalem, frequented by all sorts of celebrities and politicians. It was a high-end, exclusive access venue. It would be a great honor to host Justin and the team of *Mr. Justin Hacks*, big social media celebrities. They had hesitated to go, as they had an early flight back the next day, but who cared—they were young, rich, and famous. Besides, what if they got the chance to find the protagonist for their next viral video? You always have to be on the lookout for opportunities.

As expected, the place was packed. When word got out that *Mr. Justin Hacks* would be there, few could resist the curiosity to be close to the celebrity of the moment, hoping to snap a couple of selfies with Justin or maybe appear as extras in the next big release on his YouTube channel, where some poor devil would be shamed in exchange for millions of likes and views.

They were given one of the best spots, in a private area, with treatment befitting celebrities. Champagne on the house. Justin and Tim drank like kings, watching with pride as their girlfriends, Delia and Susan, danced suggestively for them, making out to the beat of the electronic music.

Hours passed, and the celebration grew more intense, now accompanied by pretentious flatterers. Drinks and food kept appearing in abundance. A voluptuous brunette with a tiny miniskirt and the bearing of a seductive oriental princess, whom Justin had been eyeing for a while, seized the moment when a slow, romantic song came on. She wrapped her arms around Justin's neck, pulling him into a rhythmic carnal desire, taking advantage of a momentary lapse in Delia's attention.

Justin did little to resist the insinuation, entranced by the beauty of the woman who ensnared him, who, like a witch, now enveloped him in a cloud of pheromones.

This joy was abruptly interrupted when, in a fit of jealousy, Delia threw the contents of a glass she was holding over them, demanding that Susan accompany her to the bathroom to complain about the adulterer, not without first shouting in his face, "You disgusting pig!"

With obvious regret for having to set aside the beautiful enchantress, Justin tried to stop his girlfriend to explain himself, but in the sea of people, it was impossible to catch up with her. He tried to push through, but fans who recognized him held him back, eager to touch their idol and ask for a selfie. When he finally reached the area where the women's bathrooms were, he no longer saw her. He glanced in and called her name a couple of times. He decided to wait nearby but ended up lost in the dark, tumultuous forest of human figures.

It was then that something yanked him violently into a corner. A shadowy figure loomed before him, forming the silhouette of a large human. He had no time to react. It all happened in an instant. The last thing he felt was a soothing, drowsy veil descending over him.

Justin slowly emerged from his sluggish stupor. His ears rang, his head spun; everything blurred together. *"What just happened?"* he wondered. Sharp stabs at his temples signaled an impending headache. He struggled to focus. Darkness surrounded him. Was he staring at the night sky? He soon realized he was lying on his back on a dusty surface. Panic set in when he noticed his hands, resting on his stomach, and his feet were tightly bound.

"What the hell?!" He squirmed, trying to free himself. His vision remained hazy, and panic surged until he froze at the sound of distant, menacing laughter.

"Who's there?" he called out, his voice trembling.

The laughter morphed into a mocking cackle. Justin's voice caught in his throat; only pitiful sobs escaped, fueling the macabre amusement.

"Who are you?! What do you want?!" he screamed, desperation tightening his chest.

"My dear Justin. You have no idea how long I've wanted to meet you," came the answer, accompanied by a chilling laugh. "You could say I'm karma personified. Ever heard of karma, Justin? I doubt it. Scum like you don't know such lofty concepts. But don't worry, I'll explain soon enough," a deep male voice mocked, emerging from a shadowy figure standing nearby.

A towering man dressed in a monk-like black tunic pulled back his hood, revealing a ghastly, corpse-like face. Justin's soul seemed to flee his body; he couldn't breathe. After what felt like an eternity, he forced out a scream of terror.

"Calm down, little buddy. Behave, and I won't hurt you. Actually, I brought you here for a little fun," the man chuckled.

"Tell me what you want! What is this? What do you want from me?" Justin pleaded, trembling.

"I already told you. We're here to have fun. Isn't that what you do—entertain people?"

Justin stared, blank-faced, utterly confused. His body trembled. Finally, with great effort, he whispered, "Where are we?"

The giant man yanked him up by the collar like a rag doll.

"Welcome to *Akeldama*, better known as the Field of Blood," the figure announced, pointing into the distance. Despite the darkness, faint city lights and the crescent moon's glow revealed a desolate, rugged landscape, bordered by trees and bushes. The man gestured toward what appeared to be ancient walls or the ruins of a monastery. The air felt cold and oppressive. Despair weighed heavily on Justin.

"You're a worldly man, Justin. Surely you've heard of *Akeldama*?" Justin shook his head hesitantly, like a student afraid of giving the wrong answer.

The hooded man laughed again.

"Well, let me educate you. We're in the valley of Hinnom, also known as the Valley of Hell. This place has a grim history of betrayal and damnation. Cursed land. Over two thousand years ago, priests bought this field with thirty pieces of silver. Do you know where that money came from? A man named Judas Iscariot betrayed another for those coins, a man who was later crucified. Overcome by guilt, Judas returned the blood money to the temple and hung himself. The priests deemed the coins too tainted for the treasury, so they bought this cursed field, a cemetery for the unworthy. From then on, it's been known as the Field of Blood, where the soil is stained red, and those buried here are forever damned." His voice dripped with malice as he finished the story.

Justin trembled, too terrified to speak. His mind screamed, *"What does any of this have to do with me?"* The man seemed to sense his thoughts.

"I'm bringing you to the last tourist destination you'll ever visit, you miserable wretch. Ironic, isn't it? You're going to be buried alive here, in the cursed lands of *Akeldama*," the man spat, his voice seething with hatred.

Justin screamed in terror as the man delivered a brutal punch to his stomach, doubling him over and sending him crashing to the ground. As Justin sobbed uncontrollably, the man tore a piece of duct tape from his tunic and slapped it over Justin's mouth. Then, grabbing him by the feet, he dragged him across the ground.

"Do you see that?" the man pointed to a large, transparent box.

"That's what we call *Snow White's coffin*." He let out a crazed laugh before hoisting Justin up like a sack of potatoes and placing him inside. Nearby was a massive trench.

"That's your grave," the man sneered.

Justin thrashed and pleaded, offering everything he owned for his life. Too bad his words were muffled by the tape. The man with the cadaveric face calmly secured the transparent lid over the box with heavy clasps, ignoring Justin's frantic struggles. He leaned down, pushing the box into the shallow trench, then shone a flashlight on Justin's petrified face, letting out another hysterical laugh.

"Bon voyage. Give my regards to Judas."

He started shoveling reddish dirt onto the box.

"*Requiescat in pace*," the man whispered.

After tossing the last pile, he removed his mask, wiped the sweat from his brow, and raised his left hand to check his Apple Watch. It was 11:58 p.m. He set a timer for three minutes. Watching the countdown, Yaakov felt a rare satisfaction.

Revenge, pure and unfiltered, was finally his. The satisfaction of fulfilled revenge brought him an almost transcendent ecstasy. At last, someone delivered justice to that disrespectful, hateful, and insufferable influencer who dared to humiliate him in front of the world; him, a senior Mossad agent privy to state secrets and involved in missions reminiscent of James Bond films. What he inflicted on Justin would undoubtedly deliver the effects of what is often called shock therapy.

"He won't dare mock even himself again," he mused with a trace of humor.

He thought back to his days as a *katsa* when he used *Snow White's coffin* as a psychological terror method. He had it down to an art—three minutes. No more, no less. The trench wasn't fully covered, and the coffin had small holes to allow air in, preventing asphyxiation. This was terror at its finest, and in *Akeldama* of all places—a land brimming with dark myths and legends.

Before three minutes had passed, he put on the mask again and hurriedly began clearing the dirt off the coffin. His goal was to release Justin immediately. He planned to greet him by saying, "*Rise from the dead. Make the most of this second chance*," and then put him to sleep, but this time with a sedative, not formaldehyde. He would leave him at the entrance of his hotel.

The poor devil would never know what happened to him and would return to his country a changed man. Maybe he'd even change the theme of his YouTube channel.

When he finished clearing the dirt and looked at the coffin's cover, he was struck dumb by what he saw. It was something he had never seen before. The coffin was empty.

He shone his flashlight into the transparent coffin, making sure the darkness wasn't playing tricks on him. Justin wasn't inside. He couldn't believe it. He quickly removed the clasps and lifted the cover. There was nothing. He started feeling the inside like a blind man searching for an object in desperation. He ripped off his mask and tunic, throwing them violently to the side. He was drenched in sweat, his heart pounding.

"What the hell is going on?!" he exclaimed, clutching his head.

"What kind of sick joke is this?" he shouted.

"Justin! Justin! Where have you gone, you son of a bitch? Stop messing around because when I find you, you'll wish you were never born."

He thought Justin was playing a prank, but soon realized that was impossible—he had planned everything, and no one else knew about his secret mission. His anger shifted to an agonizing worry. He began searching the entire perimeter, calling out desperately for the YouTuber. No one answered. Only the faint wind responded with a desolate tone and eerie night sounds. He returned several times to the grave, even pulling the coffin from the trench, thinking it might have broken and buried Justin under the dirt. He started digging frantically with his hands, like a dog unearthing a bone. He refused to use the shovel, fearing it might injure Justin if he was beneath the ground.

"Justin! Justin! Can you hear me? Answer me, for God's sake!" he screamed, his voice cracking. It was no use. "*Stop digging*," his bloody fingers seemed to say. It was impossible for Justin to have sunk or moved. Not even in the finest sand could that have happened.

Confusion and desperation gnawed at him like a pack of rabid dogs. He began running wildly, venturing further into *Akeldama*. All he found was more desolation and darkness. He thought he saw a cluster of shadows in a corner, but he had to stay calm. He couldn't act recklessly. The first thing he accepted was that Justin's escape from the coffin was impossible. He would have noticed. Not even Houdini in his prime could have pulled off such an escape.

But where was Justin? What happened? Had he been swallowed by the cursed lands of *Akeldama*? Impossible.

The so-called curses were nothing but stupid legends, even blasphemies.

"*Think!*" he demanded of himself. Under no circumstances could he ask for help. He couldn't risk involving Yatom, or he'd end up in prison, accused of kidnapping and forced disappearance, a crime against humanity.

"What do I do?" he asked the waning moon, its faint light barely illuminating the scene. He returned to his car, hidden among nearby weeds. He guzzled a bottle of water and reclined in his seat. He did some breathing exercises to calm down. He decided to make one last search, which lasted until after three in the morning. A call from Abigail interrupted him; she was worried about Yaakov's late return. It wasn't like him to stay out so late.

"Sorry, love. I lost track of time, catching up with old friends," he said, faking enjoyment.

The search was over. There was nothing more he could do. In this type of mission, they often went too far with the target. There was nothing left but to accept the losses and act as if nothing had happened. After all, he had rid himself of the enemy, the so-called terrorist threatening his peace of mind.

Could he pretend nothing had happened? He had done so all his life.

Upon arriving at his apartment, he made as little noise as possible to avoid waking Abigail. He quietly hid his things and threw his dirty clothes into a trash bag for disposal the next day. Then, Abigail's voice called him.

"What are you doing, darling? Come to bed," she said suggestively.

"I'll be there in a minute. I just need to shower quickly. I smell like cigarette smoke from all the smokers on the terrace."

What he really wanted to wash off was the sweat mixed with the reddish soil of *Akeldama*, which, when it swirled down the drain, looked like blood. His mind was in turmoil.

"*Where the hell was Justin? No one just disappears.*" Had the demon of his rage made him see hallucinations, like a man delirious from thirst in the desert? Was he going mad?

He finished his shower and, to escape the flood of thoughts, took a double dose of the sleeping pills his therapist had prescribed. Abigail's romantic intentions were frustrated the moment Yaakov hit the pillow.

Thursday, August eleventh. Yaakov woke late. Despite sleeping over eight hours, he felt unrested. His sleep was disturbed by confusing dreams he couldn't fully recall, except for one: the recurring image of a shadow perched in a giant tree, watching him with reproach. It unsettled him even in wakefulness. He hoped yesterday had been a nightmare, but little by little, reality set in. He rubbed his forehead. A splitting headache tortured him. He looked for Abigail, but she had already left for work.

Checking his watch, he realized it had died, as had his phone. Odd, since both had been charged before bed. He felt feverish. A cold shower barely shook off the lethargy. He dressed sluggishly, checked his phone again, but it wasn't fully charged. He went to the kitchen for breakfast.

Turning on the small television, he tried to catch the news to see if there was anything about Justin's disappearance. He left it on while preparing coffee and scrambling eggs. Suddenly, the television erupted with screams. He looked up to see a grotesque horror movie playing.

"I thought I put on the news," he muttered.

Strangely, every channel he turned to was playing horror movies. He finally turned off the television after seeing an extremely realistic scene of a man's head being smashed with a hammer.

"Just what I needed," he grumbled.

He was sipping his coffee, regaining some calm, when his phone rang. The number displayed was strange: *666-666-666*. He ignored it. It was probably a scam or unwanted promotion, as it always happened with those unrecognized, random phone numbers. He was about to call Abigail when the same number rang again. Hesitating, he answered. A voice on the other end left him frozen.

"Yaakov! Help me, for the love of God! Get me out of here!" it cried, full of terror.

"Who is this?" Yaakov demanded.

"It's Justin! Get me out of this hell you put me in!" the voice shouted.

His face paled. For a moment, Yaakov doubted, but then he realized: Justin was playing a cruel prank in retaliation. The demon of uncontrollable rage possessed him once again.

"Listen, you son of a bitch! I'll find you, no matter where you are. I have the resources and the knowledge. This time, I'll dismember you and feed your remains to dogs. You hear me?!"

"Please, Yaakov, forgive me! Just get me out—" The line went silent after a scream, followed by the sound of a chainsaw and guttural laughter. The call cut off.

"Justin?! Are you there?"

He tried calling back, but the phone didn't even ring. Rage took over him, his body trembling. He was convinced someone was playing a cruel prank that had now crossed all boundaries. What happened next hit him like a bucket of cold water. A message arrived with a video file attached. When he opened it, he saw a bewildered Justin walking down a dimly lit corridor, resembling a mausoleum. The space was cold and minimalist, bathed in pale tones. Out of nowhere, a man dressed as a courier appeared, holding a box the size of a shoebox.

"Are you Mr. Justin Richards?"

"Yes…"—he replied, confused, hesitant.

"It's for you. The sender says it's a surprise you'll love," the courier said with a manic grin. Yaakov's blood ran cold when the man glanced at the camera, winking and flashing a macabre smile. Justin, still puzzled, began opening the box.

"But… it's empty," he said, frowning.

"Look closer," the courier suggested, barely containing laughter. He shot another glance at the camera, his eyes signaling that something dreadful was about to unfold. Justin leaned into the box, and without warning, a thunderous explosion erupted. A cannonball blasted out, smashing Justin's head like a watermelon. The image was surreal. Blood splattered everywhere. What remained was a grotesque stump—his jaw and tongue barely hanging. Despite this, Justin emitted awful, guttural wails. The courier collapsed to the ground, convulsing with laughter. Yaakov stood frozen, unable to comprehend the horror. The video ended. His breath quickened. His vision blurred. He stumbled toward the couch and sat down with difficulty. He took deep breaths, trying to calm himself when his phone rang again.

This time, it was a video call from an unknown number. He rejected it, but it rang once more. Trembling, he answered. It was impossible—there was Justin, whole, as if he had respawned in a video game.

"Yaakov, please, don't hang up!" Justin cried, tears streaming down his face.

"Help me, please. Get me out of this infernal nightmare. They're torturing me in unimaginable ways!"

Yaakov stared, speechless, his eyes welling up at the sight.

"Where are you?! Tell me where you are!" he managed to ask, his voice desperate.

"I have no fucking idea! You're the one who brought me here! You know exactly where I am!"

Yaakov was struck silent, his mind racing. Then, on the video, a shadowy figure loomed over Justin, snatching the phone as he screamed in terror.

"Hello, Yaakov. Want to see something hilarious?" A grotesque face appeared, its mouth oozing pus, revealing rotten teeth and gums infested with worms. Its voice gurgled like someone struggling to clear their throat. A force took hold of Yaakov, compelling him to watch. Despite his urge to hang up, he couldn't.

"Watch closely, my friend. You'll love this little prank," it cackled, its laughter sounding like a demented cartoon dog.

The video shifted. Justin was tied to a chair in what appeared to be an ancient, crumbling temple. He struggled against the restraints. Suddenly, a beautiful naked woman stood before him, her voice dripping with seduction.

"Justin, I'm your biggest fan, and I'd love to suck your dick. Would you like that?"

Justin hesitated, didn't know how to react or what to say. As the woman began to slide her hand along Justin's inner thigh, another naked woman appeared from behind, carrying a bucket filled with molten metal. She smiled at the camera, discreetly signaling to Yaakov to pay attention. With terrifying precision, she flipped the bucket over Justin's head. His screams were unbearable. The metal began seeping through his flesh, melting away his skin and exposing his bones. With superhuman effort, he managed to stand up and began running all over the place, screaming in pain and trying to get the bucket off him, while his entrails spilled onto the floor as he writhed in agony. The sight was horrifying. Yaakov had witnessed gut-wrenching images of dead enemies before, but nothing compared to what he was seeing now. The women embraced, laughing hysterically. The video cut back to the grotesque face, now howling with uncontrollable laughter.

"How about that, Yaakov? I think this video is going to get me a million subscribers."

Yaakov slammed the phone down, smashing it to pieces. His smartwatch buzzed immediately with an alert. It was another message. He barely glanced at the first image: Justin's face, mangled, his eyes hanging from their sockets. He tore the watch off and stomped it as if crushing a venomous spider. Suddenly, the kitchen TV turned on, Justin's pleading voice echoing through the room. Yaakov yanked the TV from the wall, hurling it across the room. The sixty-inch screen in the living room was next, blasting disturbing screams. In a frenzy, Yaakov grabbed an aluminum coat rack and shattered the screen, destroying the infernal device. He kept smashing it, shouting in fury, demanding to be left in peace.

At that moment, Abigail returned home, and upon opening the door, she found the chaos Yaakov had caused. The first thing she saw was the destruction in the kitchen. Terrified, she covered her mouth with both hands. Hearing the shouts and violent grunts from inside the house, her chest tightened as if it would burst. Her first thought was that it might be a burglar or a terrorist seeking revenge against Yaakov.

She was about to run out, but she recognized his voice. She approached the living room and found him furiously smashing the television with the battered coat rack, like a lumberjack chopping down a tree.

"Yaakov! Stop! What are you doing?" she screamed.

He turned to look at her with a wild expression. For a moment, it seemed as though he didn't recognize her. He stood frozen, sweat dripping down his face, the veins on his neck and forehead bulging.

"What's going on?" Abigail demanded, her face pale as a ghost.

Yaakov struggled to find words. Even if he wanted to explain, it seemed impossible. He didn't know where to start.

"I'm under attack. It's revenge! All the electronic devices are hacked. I know this might sound insane, but I'll explain later. For now, I need to get out of here. I have to do something."

Abigail stared at him, barely recognizing the man who now seemed like a stranger. She had never seen him like this.

"What are you talking about?" She paused, thinking.

"Is this why Yatom has been looking for you?" she asked, frowning.

"What do you mean?"

"I had to come find you because Yatom called me. He said he urgently needed to speak with you. He's been trying to reach you for hours. You weren't answering his calls, texts, or emails. He's worried sick. I've been trying to reach you too, for hours."

Yaakov stood still, lost in thought. He assumed Yatom must have already been alerted to Justin's disappearance. Given that, it was likely the police, following protocol since it involved an American citizen, had informed Mossad. His old comrade was the only one who could help him figure out what was happening. His thoughts were interrupted when Abigail's phone rang. She answered quickly. It was Yatom.

"Yes, I'm with him now. I'll put him on."

"It's Yatom. He wants to talk to you," she said, handing him the phone. Yaakov hesitated briefly before taking it.

"Yatom, brother, I need your help!"

"I need your help! Please! Make this hell stop, this endless, cyclical torture!" Justin screamed from the other end of the line. His voice was soon drowned by screeching mechanical noises and sinister laughter. Yaakov recoiled, staring at the phone as his hands began to tremble.

"No... No, it can't be!" he shouted, smashing Abigail's phone against the floor and stomping on it like he was crushing a venomous insect. She watched him, horrified.

"Don't tell me you're part of this too?" he demanded, clenching his jaw, his fist tightening.

"What are you talking about? Have you lost your mind?" Abigail cried, her face contorted in anguish, tears streaming down her cheeks.

"Please, Yaakov, tell me what's happening so I can help you."

Yaakov gripped his head with both hands, writhing, pacing back and forth.

"I must find him! It's the only way to end this," he muttered to himself.

"Find who?" Abigail asked desperately, helpless as she watched him unravel. She was overwhelmed with worry, unable to recognize the man she loved. He looked at her with vacant eyes.

"I need to return to *Akeldama*."

Without another word, he bolted to his room. From his secret stash, he grabbed a few belongings, including his gun. He snatched his car keys.

"Where are you going?"

"I'm sorry. I'll explain later. I have to end this, or they'll never leave me in peace."

Abigail tried to stop him, confused and crying, pleading for an explanation, but it was no use.

Yaakov drove recklessly through the main streets of Jerusalem, heading toward *Akeldama*, the Field of Blood. He paid no attention to pedestrians or traffic lights; those concerns were a distant blur. As he neared his destination, the car's sound system suddenly blasted at full volume. A grim voice filled the air, asking a disturbing question.

"This is going to thrill you, Yaakov. Have you ever wondered what would happen if you plugged an air compressor into someone's rectum? Let's find out." A harsh laugh followed.

"Yaakov! Make it stop! I beg you," Justin's voice cried out, followed by an agonizing scream. Yaakov frantically tried to turn off the radio, but the volume only increased, causing him to lose control and swerve off the road. He crashed into the corner of an old building. Fortunately, the impact wasn't severe, but he hit his head, and blood trickled down his forehead. As he regained his senses and saw bystanders beginning to gather, he grabbed his belongings, abandoned the vehicle, and continued on foot. The place was less than a kilometer away.

At that time of day, the area was usually crowded with tourists, so he couldn't use the main entrance. He circled around and took a shortcut through an abandoned, rocky path that led to the southern slope of the Valley of Hinnom. He moved stealthily until he reached the back of the Monastery of Saint Onuphrius, built on the site of an ancient Christian cemetery.

The sky darkened with ominous clouds. The wind howled with eerie whispers, as if a storm was imminent. By now, Yaakov had completely lost track of time. He felt as if he were being transported to a distant, ancient era. A desolate silence hung in the air, and a wave of dizziness from the blow to his head swept over him. He touched the lump on his forehead; it had stopped bleeding. When he was certain no one was around, he descended a small slope toward the spot where he had buried Justin. The place seemed deserted. Not a soul in sight. Maybe the threat of the storm had driven everyone indoors. It was better this way.

There lay the trench he had dug to bury Justin. He pulled a collapsible shovel from his backpack and began digging again, convinced Justin must have fallen into a tunnel. The area was filled with ancient caves, rumored to have been used by early Christians hiding from Roman persecution. He even remembered hearing about an underground church nearby. Perhaps hell itself had swallowed Justin, he thought.

He dug frantically, but the deeper he went, the harder the ground became. Lightning flashed, and strange whispers surrounded him, voices just beyond perception. Yaakov glanced around but saw only desolation. He kept digging, directionless, like a shipwrecked man lost at sea. The trench grew wider, but there was still no sign of Justin. Desperation clawed at him. Sweat and red earth clung to his face, giving him the appearance of a man encased in a scab of blood.

"Justin! Where are you?" he yelled in desperation, like a father losing sight of his child in a crowd. Mocking laughter filled his mind. He dug harder and faster until the shovel snapped, and a sharp piece of the handle pierced his hand. He cried out in pain, "Damn it!" Instantly, a thunderous laugh echoed around him.

"Shut up once and for all, you son of a bitch! Show yourself!" he shouted, drawing his gun and firing blindly at unseen enemies until the magazine emptied.

"Yaakov! I'm here!" a voice called from afar.

"Justin?"

Yaakov climbed out of the trench and tried to locate the source of the voice, which had now turned into a pitiful wail. It came from near the base of the Monastery of Saint Onuphrius, close to a massive stone wall, where Yaakov spotted Justin standing at a small entrance, signaling for help. Suddenly, an anthropomorphic figure dragged him into the building. Yaakov ran toward the old structure with all his might, but the more he ran, the further away the monastery seemed. His steps grew heavier, and the wound on his hand bled uncontrollably.

Akeldama was cast into shadow under a darkening sky. Justin's cries echoed through the heavy, oppressive air, which smelled of stagnant water. Like an octopus releasing ink into the sea, a strong gust whipped up a dust storm that swallowed everything in sight. Lost and frustrated, Yaakov pushed on, but the ghostly taunts became clearer, turning his frustration into rage. Fueled by adrenaline, he sprinted faster, only to be stopped violently when he tripped over a large rock and fell flat on his face. He rolled several meters before coming to a stop, feeling as though he'd been beaten by a lynch mob.

It took a moment to recover, and through sobs, he tried to stand, but something held him paralyzed.

In the distance, a vision unfolded like a medieval painting, with apocalyptic religious imagery in intense, haunting tones. He saw the silhouette of a man lowering himself from a tree. As soon as his feet touched the ground, a thunderous crack of lightning reverberated. The man approached until he stood close to Yaakov. His features were obscured, but his ancient attire was vaguely visible in the shadows. Everything was shrouded in darkness. Lying on the ground, Yaakov raised his left hand and, in a trembling voice, called out to Justin.

The man responded, *"Justin is no more and never will be. The more you search for him, the more lost you will become. You made a choice you could have avoided, but like many men, using me as a shameful example, your greed to satisfy your ego, your thirst to indulge your basest instincts, consumed you. A wise man once said, 'It is better to turn the other cheek.' How different humanity would be if we had listened. You took your revenge, using the lands of Akeldama as your instrument—a field of blood, seeded with betrayal and watered with vengeance. Now, you will reap the harvest. The exaltation you felt from revenge is yours to live with for the rest of your days, for that fruit is now part of you."*

As he finished speaking, the man pointed at Yaakov, and the ground began to tremble.

Yaakov felt like he was being electrocuted as the earth split open beneath him, dragging him into the bowels of *Akeldama*. When he hit bottom, he found himself in a dimly lit cave chamber. Candles and torches faintly illuminated the walls, which were lined with funerary niches. In front of him loomed a massive ossuary wall, stacked high with thousands of bones. Whispers, murmurs, and laughter echoed like a twisted chorus in a stadium of the dead. The atmosphere was suffocating, thick with the stench of decay. The bones began to rattle, producing a drumming sound.

"Welcome home," said a ghostly voice. Yaakov lay on his back, unable to move. His body felt shattered, and he could only slightly turn his head. He locked eyes with Justin, whose vacant gaze and cadaverous face sent waves of horror through him. The lacerations on Justin's chest resembled ancient hieroglyphics carved into stone. Yaakov was too terrified to react before an avalanche of skeletons buried him, their bones piercing his flesh like venomous stingers. The pain was indescribable.

Yaakov was later admitted to a psychiatric hospital, his mental health in shambles. Diagnosed with schizophrenic psychosis, doctors couldn't predict whether he'd ever regain emotional stability. For now, discharge was out of the question. Police and two Mossad agents, Yatom and Biton, had found Yaakov at the monastery's foot, rolling on the ground and screaming incoherently. His appearance was horrifying—his clothes were torn, and his face and hands were covered in blood. He looked like a walking scab, much of it due to the red earth clinging to his body. With great effort, Yaakov managed to recognize Yatom and pleaded for help.

He was first taken to a hospital, where he confessed to his friend that he had orchestrated Justin's kidnapping and disappearance, driven by revenge.

"I buried him in *Akeldama*," he repeated insistently. Despite days of intense searching, the police found not the slightest trace of Justin. At first, Yatom found his former colleague's version of events believable, as the pieces of his vengeful attitude seemed to fit together. However, the subsequent appearance of a video showing Justin leaving the bar that fateful night, accompanied by a mysterious woman dressed in black—whom they still had not managed to identify—cast doubt on Yaakov's account.

Yaakov's story was ultimately dismissed when doctors advised his admission to a psychiatric hospital due to recurring delusions. He had destroyed the television in his room, smashed medical devices, and broken visitors' cell phones, claiming Justin appeared in videos as the star of hellish hidden camera shows.

Abigail, heartbroken, watched as the man she once loved became unrecognizable, his only words echoing, "*Sometimes, it's better to turn the other cheek.*"

THE EMPRESS OF CLAY

I remain here, and I will continue like this for the rest of my days, purging my sentence in this dreadful prison. It's a glimpse of what awaits me in hell if I don't manage to amend my ways in this Dantesque reformatory. Though my cell is spacious, and I enjoy comforts that other prisoners envy, the conditions are worthy of a horror film in every sense. I know I shouldn't complain; I brought this upon myself, and I've come to terms with that. Still, I believe anyone in my position would have broken in this place. I nearly did. But I don't want to get ahead of myself. This isn't a complaint, but a testimony—my version of events that I wish to share.

My cellmates are grotesque, deformed, monstrous beings. At first, their voices were unbearable hoarse growls and laughter that sounded like the rumbling of an empty stomach, filling me with revulsion. When I first heard them speak, I couldn't understand a word, as they spoke in a dialect that seemed utterly foreign. Perhaps my disoriented mind was clouding my comprehension. Only when I managed to calm down and focus did I begin to understand them.

There's another aspect of this prison I haven't mentioned: the utter darkness. I live in it constantly, twenty-four hours a day. Light, color, shape, and, most of all, the beauty of the outside world now exist only as memories. An additional, irreversible sentence—a consequence of my selfish, foolish outbursts. A decision made that cannot be appealed in this world.

Over time, I've learned to coexist with the inhabitants of this dark world, to accept them for what they are. Or rather, it's more accurate to say I must accept myself for what I've always been. My pride remains something I need to work on. I've even begun what, in a normal world, could be considered a relationship with one of them. I met him during the first few months after I was transported to this infernal place. A couple of weeks ago, I started allowing him to visit me daily. Yes, even in this prison, there is surprising flexibility regarding visits. Did I mention it's a co-ed facility? Well, that's not relevant right now.

By the way, his name is Gael. I enjoy our conversations. I can't deny he has a kind heart. Under different circumstances, I might easily fall in love with him, but a part of me resists.

There's a barrier, a concrete wall, that I'm desperately trying to tear down. For anyone else, this wouldn't be an issue, but for me, raised with an idealized Greek concept of beauty, it's nearly insurmountable.

A few days ago, Gael confessed his love and even tried to kiss me. I must admit, I reacted like a frightened animal, even going so far as to ask him to leave and never return. But I regretted it almost immediately and apologized for my irrational behavior. Of course, he understood, which is why I say he's a remarkable person. He knows my limitations.

Now, you may wonder: what's stopping me from breaking down that wall and giving myself to him? The answer is simple. Gael is a monstrosity—a deformed creature, his appearance similar to that of a leper. His nose has no cartilage, and his face is covered in blisters and sores. Perhaps I'm exaggerating, but that's the image seared into my mind from our first encounter. Although those lesions aren't as pronounced anymore, it seems they're healing. But even so, I can't imagine being physically intimate with him. It pains me to admit it, but the mere thought of it is enough to snuff out the faint ember of what was once my fiery sexual desire, smothered by a cold polar wind.

I met him in what some might call a hospital, before my imprisonment in this world of darkness. When I was first dragged into this hellish city, its inhabitants regarded me with suspicion, thinking I had lost my mind. I behaved like a wild animal, completely out of control, desperate to escape. After wandering the streets in such a pitiful state, I eventually collapsed. That's when I found myself in what resembled a sanatorium.

When I awoke from the drug-induced stupor brought on by my captors, I thought, for a moment, that it had all been a terrible nightmare. But soon I had to face the grim reality. Gael approached to help me, but his appearance horrified me. Despite his efforts to calm me and explain the situation, his presence, like that of everyone around me, only deepened my fear and disgust. Ironically, it was he who ended up saving my life, showing genuine concern for my well-being.

But how did I end up in this world and in the prison I've described? That's my story. I'll try to be brief and avoid irrelevant details.

My name is Veronica Kelly-Cruz. I was born in Riverside, California, and raised in a middle-class family that rose to success thanks to my parents' professional growth. I am the youngest of three siblings. My father's side is Irish, while my mother's heritage is Cuban. My paternal grandparents were originally from Cork, Ireland. My mother was born in Havana,

Cuba, and fled with her family to Florida. When it was time for her to attend university, she moved to California, where she met and fell in love with my father. Their relationship was seen as something straight out of a movie, thanks to their striking physical appearances.

My father, an imposing figure, stood at nearly six-foot-three, with blonde hair, blue eyes that reflected the Caribbean sea, sharp but gentle features, and a square jaw reminiscent of an ancient Viking warrior. His athletic build, shaped by his days as a defensive player on the university's football team, added to his commanding presence.

My mother, though much shorter, radiated natural beauty. Her olive skin highlighted her delicate, doll-like features—almond-shaped eyes, exquisite lips, and jet-black hair as straight and smooth as silk. My father often compared her figure to that of a Roman goddess.

Among my two brothers, I was the most fortunate in terms of inheriting this beauty. Like my father, my eyes stood out, and I shared some of his height. As for the rest of my appearance, you could say I was an enhanced reflection of my mother.

For my parents, who were obsessed with beauty and appearance, I was a divine gift, especially to my father, who had a passion for Greco-Roman history. He would tell me stories about the ancient Greeks' obsession with physical beauty.

From a young age, I was entered into children's beauty pageants, where I consistently won, as I did in school competitions. My name became synonymous with *beauty queen*. Naturally, during my school years, I was always pursued by admirers, some of whom even fought for my attention. I had the luxury of choosing the most handsome, accomplished, and financially secure suitors.

I learned to capitalize on my beauty, gradually mastering the art of manipulation. This skill helped me become a powerful woman, as doors opened effortlessly for me. I can confidently say that the stories I heard as a child about the turbulent romances and betrayals of the gods in Greek mythology influenced my professional ambitions. In some ways, I even experienced them firsthand. It's unfortunate that I ignored the parts where beauty led to the downfall of many.

Was I obsessed with my appearance? Absolutely, and to some degree, I still am. By now, you've probably realized where this obsession stems from. Much of the blame lies with my mother—may God bless her soul.

Over time, with our improving financial situation, she became obsessed with beauty treatments. She spent thousands on them and even dabbled in esoteric practices, particularly

Santería, which she both practiced and revered. Despite my father's strong objections—being a devout Catholic—my mother's strong character and her seductive charm (which my father sarcastically referred to as having him under a spell) always won him over. He had no choice but to tolerate what he considered to be the work of the devil. In the end, I think he was right, because it was *Santería* that opened the doors of hell for me.

After graduating from law school, I moved to Dallas and secured a position at one of the city's most prestigious law firms. I specialized in corporate and real estate law. In a short time, I became a partner. I billed my clients millions, which quickly made me a powerful and ruthless young lawyer. My legal team crushed competitors in court. Today, I'm not ashamed to admit that, in addition to my intelligence, I also relied heavily on my most potent weapon to reach the top. It wasn't just my beauty, but the combination of it with my sexual allure, which I used to sway wills, close multimillion-dollar deals, and even influence judges to rule in my favor. This same charm helped me keep the most handsome and powerful men at my feet like loyal servants.

By now, you might be thinking certain things, but let me stop you right there: No, I'm not a prostitute. I didn't recklessly throw myself at anyone who crossed my path like some nymphomaniac. My sexual encounters—and I emphasize *encounters*—were with men of significant influence in the financial, political, and even religious spheres. These encounters were exchanges, in which, in return for something, my occasional lovers received an experience reserved only for kings and high dignitaries. It's something men have done for millennia, yet they're often glorified for it, while women are branded with the scarlet letter of a whore.

Few people understand the profound power of possessing a woman like me. It drove more than one man mad. My beauty was such that, if I were a character in Greek mythology, I could have easily seduced Zeus himself and driven his wife, Hera, away. Even Aphrodite would have been no match for me.

I have a confession. If any of you are psychologists, you might diagnose me as a megalomaniac. But honestly, I couldn't care less what anyone thinks right now. I need to say this. More than once, I've believed I was the reincarnation of Queen Cleopatra.

The first step toward my downfall began when I met the man who lured me into the abyss of love. He was a powerful real estate investor who, beyond his physical perfection, radiated magnetic charisma. With him, I felt whole. For the first time, my sexuality wasn't transactional. I lost myself in hours of orgasmic labyrinths. We discussed wedding plans on several occasions, but those dreams drained away in the cesspool of infidelity. I don't even want to remember his name. *Damnatio memoriae.* I condemn him to oblivion.

Like a page torn from a classic romance, he left me for the fleeting sparkle of youth and fresher beauty. I was shattered. My pride and self-esteem were brutally crushed. For the first time, I felt ugly, vulnerable.

Things worsened when I realized something that triggered irrational terror and sent me spiraling into the dark world I now inhabit. From that moment, time became my worst enemy. I was no longer young. I was nearing thirty-three. The sands in my biological hourglass were running out. I began noticing the first wrinkles, varicose veins, and the omnipresent threat of cellulite. My breasts sagged more each day, my buttocks lost their firmness.

Panic attacks visited me nightly. I went weeks without sleep, tormented by the memory of being replaced by a younger, more beautiful rival. What good was my power if I couldn't hold onto my beauty? From then on, I knew that every romantic relationship would carry the constant threat of infidelity, of being replaced by someone younger and more attractive. Aging would strip away the power I once wielded.

My strongest currency would depreciate until it was worthless, like the Weimar Republic's doomed currency—a million-mark bill with no value at all.

I imagined myself ending my days as a decrepit old woman, wrinkled, living off past glories, condemned to be forgotten. But instead of sinking into depression, I faced my fears head-on. As the true warrior I'd always been, I vowed to do whatever it took to preserve my beauty.

Eventually, I realized I had become my mother. Like her, I was obsessed with beauty. I tried every kind of aesthetic treatment imaginable, spending hundreds of thousands on cosmetics, creams, and lotions. I became a slave to the gym. I confess I always avoided plastic surgery, seeing it as cheating—something for women who hadn't been blessed with natural beauty, like me. The losers. Surgery was a last resort, something I'd consider only after every other method had failed. I was convinced I would never need to go that far, especially when I remembered where to find the fountain of eternal youth.

As I mentioned, my mother, a devout practitioner of *Santería*, didn't rely solely on chemical beauty treatments. She also turned to natural and esoteric remedies to enhance and preserve her appearance. She underwent all kinds of rituals, dances, and hypnotic trances, drank potions made from

African herbs, prayed, and invoked ancestral deities. These practices led to intense arguments with my father, nearly driving them to divorce. She traveled the world in search of the magical element that would grant her eternal beauty and youth. She found it, but life never gave her the chance to try it.

My mother died when I was twenty-seven. She was young. Breast cancer took her, and by the time she sought treatment, it was too late. It's ironic that, in her quest for beauty, she neglected the most important thing—her health. At least she fulfilled her wish to die young and beautiful. In her final days, she revealed to me the magical secret she had discovered, one that would not only restore physical beauty but preserve it through old age.

It was something that would make her look eternally in her twenties. It was ancient clay, imbued with mysterious divinity. But to obtain it, she had to retrieve it herself. No one else could bring it to her. When she finally intended to make the journey, she was already too sick.

That secret was revealed to her by a high priestess of *Santería*, a *Babalawo*—a priest with divination powers and a practitioner of rituals. It was a mixture of earth and clay from sacred lands. *Barrosanctum* was its name. A treatment once used by the most powerful empresses of ancient Rome, including

Messalina, wife of Emperor Claudius, allowing them not only to enhance their beauty but to completely dominate their husbands, becoming the true power behind the throne. Or so I believed, until I learned more about Messalina's unfortunate fate.

The priestess warned her, with great emphasis, that this treatment was not to be used lightly, nor without understanding its properties. It required specific conditions and rituals, which my mother documented in a detailed diary. She shared all this with me, along with other *Santería* teachings, on her deathbed, so that I would be prepared if ever the time came.

Unlike my mother, I was never devoted to *Santería* or its rituals; I considered them trivial, if not outright superstitions. In my twenties, I believed that to stand out as a lawyer and become a powerful figure in the business world, I had to free myself from religious beliefs that would only serve as mental shackles to my success. I even distanced myself from Catholicism, much to my father's dismay. That's why, at the time, I dismissed the secret of *barrosanctum* as nothing more than a witch's tale. I wish I had continued thinking that way, but my obsession with beauty led me to the edges of sacrilege.

Here comes the hardest part of my story, as it reopens wounds in my soul when I recall the events that led to my downfall. What is *barrosanctum*? For those familiar with beauty treatments, it's nothing more than mud therapy—a mixture of earth, clay, and a few other ingredients combined with water to achieve aesthetic and healing benefits. But this is no ordinary mud. The earth and clay used in *barrosanctum* can only be found in a place both sacred and cursed: *Akeldama*, the *Field of Blood*, also known as the *Potter's Field*. It lies in Jerusalem, near the Valley of Hinnom.

The history of this place is steeped in betrayal and desecration. Despite knowing its background, my obsession blinded me, making me stubborn and causing me to overlook the many warnings I was given about it.

Akeldama was purchased at a terrible price—perhaps the greatest betrayal in history. The money used for it was cursed; it was the thirty pieces of silver Judas Iscariot received for betraying Jesus. According to biblical accounts, when Judas realized the enormity of his act, he tried to return the coins to the priests, but since they were considered blood money, they couldn't be placed in the temple's offering box. So, they used the coins to buy a field for burying foreigners and pilgrims. Legend has it that the blood from the thirty silver pieces cursed the field, staining its soil red.

Nine years passed after my mother's death before desperation drove me to seek *barrosanctum*. I had just turned thirty-five when I met Dante Mirren, a successful and powerful criminal lawyer. What started as a relationship of convenience soon grew into a passionate affair, softening my hardened heart. At last, after so long, I saw the possibility of falling in love again and entering a long-term relationship. But, like a lurking demon, the constant fear of being replaced by a younger, more beautiful woman began to torment me.

This fear had two facets. The first was that Dante was five years younger than me. I had always believed that women aged faster than men, and that men sought younger women as a result. In my mind, I was already losing. The second facet was that Dante was highly sought after by women and had admitted to a colorful romantic past. Though he swore he had left that life behind and now wanted stability, I knew from experience that sexual desire often overpowers reason.

Determined to eliminate any competition and remove all temptation to replace me, I resolved to make Dante fall madly in love with me and, more than that, to control him—just as the most powerful empresses of ancient Rome had done.

At the end of March 2024, despite the danger of the ongoing conflict in Israel, I decided to travel to Jerusalem to obtain the magical soil that would grant me beauty and power until death. The risk of entering a war zone seemed insignificant compared to the rewards. I reasoned that Jerusalem, being a holy city and a major tourist destination, would be shielded from bombings or terrorist attacks. Besides, I wasn't going as a tourist; I would fly in on a private plane and return as soon as I acquired what I needed.

Upon arriving in Jerusalem, my first task was to locate Ezra Jotam, a scholar mentioned in my mother's notebook. He was described as an expert in arcane knowledge, occultism, and the mysteries of *Akeldama*.

Finding him was no simple task; the address in the notebook was outdated, and years had passed since he last lived there. With the help of a few neighbors, I eventually tracked him down in the outskirts of the ancient City of David, living in a modest house nestled among cobblestone streets. Being there felt like stepping back in time. Despite his advanced age, Ezra Jotam remained a well-known figure among treasure hunters and scholars of ancient mysteries.

Ezra seemed like a character plucked from a story about wizards and sorcerers. He wore an anachronistic outfit that evoked forgotten eras. His appearance, marked by the wisdom of his years, was defined by his piercing eyes and an inquisitive yet intimidating gaze.

At first, when I mentioned *Akeldama*, he nearly threw me out of his house, reacting with fury. But when I mentioned the name of the high priestess of *Santería* my mother had spoken of, he reconsidered. A few bills helped soften him up as well.

With a trembling yet forceful voice, he urged me to abandon my quest to desecrate the lands of *Akeldama*. He confessed that although he had once benefited from the field and its so-called magical powers in his youth, he now bitterly regretted it. The price he paid was not just his peace of mind; his very soul had withered, standing now on the brink of damnation. He had evidence of many who had succumbed to the curse of *Akeldama*, suffering terrible misfortunes. He told me about a Mexican who sought revenge but ended up cursing his homeland forever.

In my arrogance, I assured him that I was immune to curses, as I knew some protective secrets from *Santería* passed down to me by my mother. The old Ezra simply laughed and said he had done his duty, and I had been warned. He would accompany me only to the entrance, but I would have to enter the field and collect the material with my own hands.

That afternoon, we headed to the agreed-upon location. Dressed in comfortable clothes and carrying two bags the size of duffel bags, I was prepared to follow Ezra's instructions.

He handed me a shovel and led me to the spot where I was to gather the key ingredient for the *barrosanctum*.

Since the area attracted tourists and visitors, drawn in part by the ancient Monastery of St. Onuphrius in the *Akeldama* region—built around the cemetery of the first Christians and foreigners—it was crucial not to arouse suspicion.

Ever the strategist, Ezra had made arrangements with a few locals to overlook our secret activities in exchange for a generous payment. Spending large sums of money didn't bother me; after all, what I was about to acquire was priceless.

I entered through the side of the old monastery, its ancient stone walls towering around me. I descended a small hill into the Valley of Hinnom. A strange sensation gripped me—a blend of fear and unease—but what stood out the most was an intense ambition, a burning desire that pushed me forward, as if I were a treasure hunter sneaking through the shadows. Looking back, I can't help but laugh at myself.

The sky, which had been clear that morning, quickly darkened with black storm clouds, and the air turned cold. The place felt desolate; the crowds had vanished. I quickened my pace, eager to finish my task and leave, but the deeper I went, the more oppressive the atmosphere became. The trees seemed to whisper strange things in the breeze, making me even more uneasy.

Finally, I reached the location Ezra had described. It was a wide, barren patch of reddish soil where others had already excavated some of the mystical material. A large trench and a broken shovel lay abandoned nearby.

Thanks to my great physical shape, I quickly filled both bags. Time slipped away as I worked. I felt light, almost euphoric, as though in a trance. Perhaps it was the effect of the soil and clay, because by the time I was done, I realized that my black clothes had turned completely red.

Despite the weight of the bags, I carried them with ease. I was exhilarated. If the dust could make me feel this powerful just by being near it, I could hardly wait to see what it would do once I applied it to my skin as part of the *Santería* ritual.

As I left, I saw Ezra sitting beneath a tree. The sun was setting over the ancient Jerusalem skyline. His face, lined with exhaustion, conveyed one final warning about the dangers of using *Akeldama's* clay. I scoffed, telling him that the land hadn't offered any resistance, and if any demons wanted to stop me, they had missed their chance. He smiled, resigned.

I called the private driver I had hired to take me back to my hotel. The next morning, at dawn, I would return to Dallas to prepare for the ritual of eternal beauty. After finishing my call, I looked around and saw that Ezra had disappeared— vanished as if into thin air. I never saw him again.

Back in Dallas, my excitement to test the barrosanctum was almost unbearable. Though I wanted to use it immediately, I decided to wait until April 8, 2024, a significant date in *Santería* that coincided with a total solar eclipse. My mother had always told me that rituals performed during an eclipse yielded enhanced results. Since Dallas would be one of the cities plunged into complete darkness during the eclipse, I was convinced it would amplify the effects of the clay of eternal beauty.

I spent the remaining week studying the prayers and instructions written in my mother's notebook, mentally preparing for the event. To my surprise, I found myself practicing *Santería* with a newfound fervor, experiencing an intoxicating sense of empowerment. If all went according to plan, I might become a regular practitioner in the future—at least, that's what I naively believed.

April 8, the day of the eclipse. I felt like a child eager to open Christmas presents. The night before, I could barely sleep. Dante was away on a business trip, which worked in my favor—no interruptions or explanations were needed.

I tossed and turned until I finally drifted off. I set the alarm for 5:00 a.m. Even though I had informed my clients and staff that I wouldn't be in that day, I wanted to make the most of the time and ensure everything was ready. The eclipse would peak at 1:42 p.m.

I spent the early hours doing yoga and meditating. As the morning progressed, I adorned my apartment with sacred objects and ritual tools, focusing on the bathroom, the designated space for the ritual. I hung religious images, scapulars, and crosses adorned with quartz and shells, filling the air with the fragrance of ceremonial herbs and burning incense.

Then came the most important part. I emptied one of the bags of *Akeldama* clay into my oval travertine and marble bathtub. I began filling it with water, adding a jug of holy water as per the instructions. I stirred the mixture with a special shovel. Everything had been prepared meticulously, just as a true professional would.

As I worked, I recited prayers and ceremonial chants, fully immersing myself in the ritual until I had a thick, reddish liquid. My heart pounded with excitement and anticipation. Watching the *barrosanctum* settle in the tub was hypnotic, almost seductive. Several times, I felt the urge to dive into it, as if it were calling to me, but I restrained myself. The eclipse was beginning, and everything had to be perfect.

The time had come. The eclipse started, and I had decided that the ritual would last until the cosmic event concluded. I lowered my naked body into the tub, sinking slowly and deliberately until I was fully submerged. The sensation of the clay covering my skin was indescribable—an enjoyable tingling unlike anything I'd ever felt. The mixture was both cool and warm, simultaneously refreshing and soothing. I made sure it covered every inch of me, even spreading it across my face like a mask. What followed was one of the most intense and extraordinary experiences of my life.

I closed my eyes and tried to relax. Soon, I began to feel a pleasurable heat spreading through my body. My heart started pounding, and I found it difficult to breathe. It was as if hundreds of hands were seductively caressing me. I felt the sensation of lips sensually licking my neck, followed by an intense caress over my breasts, which gently slid down toward my mound of Venus.

At that point, I was completely enraptured; the *barrosanctum* had become my master, and I lost myself in time and space. The more the eclipse devoured the light, the more ecstatic I became. I reached a point of such intense pleasure that I experienced an orgasm that seemed to last an eternity, and when it ended, it left me in a daze, pulling me into a deep sleep.

When I woke, the peak of the eclipse had passed; the second dawn was already breaking. I checked the time—it was 2:07 p.m. I had truly lost track of time. Feeling groggy, I decided to get out of the tub and shower to wash off the barrosanctum. I hadn't enjoyed bathing this much in a long time. The water cascading over my skin caused a subtle tingling sensation. Watching the clay dissolve in the water was eerie, as though blood were washing away.

What happened next left me in awe. I hadn't expected such immediate effects. My skin glowed, silky to the touch. My legs looked more toned, and my excitement grew as I examined my breasts—they felt firmer and rounder. When I touched my nipples, it felt as though, for a moment, I was outside my body. The clay had not only transformed my skin but also heightened my sexual desire. I hurried through the shower, eager to look at myself in the mirror.

There I stood, gazing into the tall mirror in my bathroom. It was like looking at the past. It took me a moment to recognize the beautiful woman staring back at me. It was me— Veronica—but fifteen years younger. My face looked exactly as it did when I was twenty. All the wrinkles had vanished, my lips had regained their youthful fullness, and my eyes sparkled with a vibrant glow. Every imperfection had disappeared, even the smallest scars were gone.

I couldn't contain myself—I began to cry. My hands flew to my mouth, muffling a sob of joy that only deepened as I continued to gaze at my naked body. My silhouette was perfect—sculpted, athletic, flawless. My breasts, once sagging, were now firm and lifted. My buttocks, round and smooth, appeared as though an artist had meticulously sculpted them. I looked as if Aphrodite herself had descended from her pedestal and come to life.

The emotion and happiness were overwhelming—the magical effects of the *barrosanctum* were real, not mere superstition. A wave of nostalgia hit me as I thought of my mother. How happy she would have been to witness this miracle. Sadly, she hadn't had the chance, but at least I was living this for her. I thanked her spirit for the priceless legacy she had left me. There I was—Veronica Kelly-Cruz—overflowing with eternal beauty, thanks to the ancient secrets of *Santería*. I felt invincible, my strength renewed.

Dante would be powerless before my newfound beauty. He would become obsessed, my devoted servant. My fears of being replaced by younger women had vanished, crumbling like a sandcastle. Now, he would be the one worrying about being discarded, exchanged for someone else. He would have to stay vigilant, aware of the rivals lining up to seduce me. The circle of my power was complete. Not only was I a successful lawyer and businesswoman, but now I possessed the secret of eternal beauty.

What a shock Dante was in for. I was eager to reveal myself to him. Excitement surged through me, fueled by a burning desire to be by his side. I longed to test the aphrodisiac effects of the *Barrosanctum*. I was certain he would fall at my feet.

My beloved had returned and tried to reach me several times in the last few hours, but I had turned off my phone to avoid any interruptions during the ritual. We had planned to meet at sunset in a *café* and then go to an elegant restaurant for dinner. Instead, I told him I had other matters to attend to. I suggested we have a romantic dinner at my apartment, hinting at an incredible surprise that would leave him speechless. He pressed for more details, but I let him endure the sweet torture of uncertainty.

I needed time to clear and dismantle the stage for the ritual. The source of my beauty would remain a secret, shared only between mother and daughter.

I called the most exclusive restaurant in town, *La Brasserie Étoile Dorée*, to have the finest French dishes delivered, requesting full service, including a table for two. The cost was extravagant, but money no longer mattered to me.

I searched my closet for the perfect dress—something sexy

that fit my body flawlessly—but none of them seemed right. They were unworthy. I realized I needed a complete wardrobe overhaul, an idea that thrilled me. It would be the perfect excuse to travel across Italy, seeking the best designer clothes, tailored to perfection.

But what would be the ideal attire to welcome Dante and reveal the new me? None. I decided the finest garment I could wear was the beauty of my own nakedness.

Time was running short before Dante's arrival. Everything was ready: the table set with precision. The restaurant staff had outdone themselves, decorating the center with *Château Margaux* and *Premier Grand Cru Classé*—two of the most exclusive and expensive wines. It felt as though I had brought a piece of France into my apartment.

I dimmed the lights, blending soft candlelight with the faint glow of artificial lamps. In my room, I would wait for Dante in complete darkness, lying on the bed like a seductive goddess. I wouldn't let him see me immediately; the revelation had to be slow, deliberate, shrouded in mystery.

We would skip straight to dessert—my true main course. I would let him take small bites, teasing him as he experienced the softness of my skin. He would start at my feet, guiding him slowly through the earthly paradise that was my body. In the dark, I would let him savor me in small sips, as if he were a parched man finding an oasis in the desert.

I would make him suffer just a little, and only when he was entirely under my spell would I turn on the lights. The moment would bring him to an unimaginable ecstasy, completely surrendering to our encounter. I was certain that, upon seeing me, he would be overwhelmed with such pleasure that he would spiral into madness.

I was lying on my bed when I heard the front door begin to open. Anxiety and desperation tortured me. Footsteps echoed, followed by a voice—Dante's—though at that moment, it seemed unintelligible. He was calling me from the kitchen. I guided him toward the bedroom with my voice. I heard him approaching. He was already at the door. I asked him not to turn on the lights. He said something, but I couldn't make it out; excitement had clouded my senses.

In a soft, sensual tone, I instructed him to undress and follow my lead. It was one of the conditions for the surprise I had prepared for him. I would orchestrate everything, controlling our encounter. It should be like opening a present, carefully, without tearing the wrapping. He made strange sounds, which I took as expressions of his excitement, assuming he was playing his part in the game.

He began to caress my feet slowly, his touch deliberate. I

ordered him to move over my body with restraint, forbidding any sudden moves. His rough, calloused touch surprised me, but I attributed it to my heightened sensitivity, not giving it much thought. My excitement was escalating to dangerous levels, and I wasn't sure if I could contain myself any longer. Apparently, Dante was reaching his limit as well, as his moans grew increasingly unusual.

When he started licking my breasts, the sensation was strange, though not unpleasant—until he kissed me. His lips felt different, and his breath carried a pungent odor. I recoiled slightly, but he persisted, continuing to kiss me. As I placed my hands on his back, confusion swept over me. There were odd bumps, like protruding shoulder blades, and his spine felt as if the vertebrae were about to break through his skin. Disoriented, I didn't know what to think.

I told him to stop, sensing something was terribly wrong, but Dante just ignored me. He began to penetrate me. Pain surged through me, and I demanded that he stop, but it only spurred him on. He was on top of me, letting out beastly groans. Fear gripped me. I managed to reach the bedside table and turn on the light. It wasn't Dante.

Horror consumed me as I looked at what was on top of me: a grotesque figure, a deformed face, with eyes bulging out of their sockets and an infernal grin that revealed black teeth and rotting gums. It was like seeing Jason Voorhees. I had never experienced fear of such magnitude before. I was being raped. Summoning strength from the deepest part of my being, I managed to push him away with a kick.

I began to scream, pleading for help, throwing everything within reach at him. The deformed man stood in the corner, naked; his skin looked like it had been burned with acid, and his penis was like that of a horny beast. He stood there, gesturing at me and making strange babbling sounds. I kept shouting at him, demanding he not dare come closer, but he ignored me and lunged toward me. With agility, I dodged him and, in the process, landed a strong punch to his jaw, sending him to the floor like a ragdoll.

Taking advantage of the fact that the monstrous rapist was on the ground, stunned by the blow, I ran to my closet to get dressed. I put on the first thing I could find: some jeans, a T-shirt, and my sneakers. I tied up my hair and looked for my phone to call Dante. I was stunned to realize his phone was in the room, on a small table. There it was, ringing. The first thought that crossed my mind was that the abhorrent violator had attacked him when he arrived at the apartment.

Not knowing what to do, fear paralyzed me. I tried to call 911, but I locked my phone after entering the wrong password several times due to the fear and confusion overwhelming me. Meanwhile, the man on the floor started calling my name in a trembling voice that I could barely make out: "Veronica, what's happening?" I kicked him under the ribs and ran toward the exit. I began screaming, calling for help, but what I found outside was nothing more than the reception area to hell.

The hallway was dimly lit, everything looked dull and grayish. The walls were cracked, marked with dampness and wear. The floor was covered with a layer of dust and grime. It was like being in an abandoned place where time had been merciless.

The air reeked of confinement, stale and oppressive. Though I recognized the place, it felt unfamiliar. I had the sensation of being trapped in a nightmare, desperately trying to control my consciousness as one does in such moments. But soon, I realized this was real. I wasn't dreaming.

I bolted to the left side of the hallway, where I knew the exclusive elevators for the penthouse were just a few meters away. They seemed to be working. I pressed the button frantically. As I waited, I glanced around, making sure the rapist wasn't coming after me. Finally, I unlocked my phone, and just as I started dialing 911, the elevator doors slid open. Inside, I could make out three figures.

The lighting was dim. I couldn't see their faces. At first, I hesitated, but instinct drove me inside. I begged for help, frantically telling them someone had broken into my apartment to rape me and that I didn't understand what was happening or why everything looked so wrong.

A woman reached out, placing her hand on my shoulder, speaking in a strange language. I told her I didn't understand. As she leaned closer, I saw her face—her skin was transparent, revealing her facial muscles and greenish veins as if she had no skin at all. Her eyeballs were exposed, as was the cartilage of her nose. Despite having lips, her teeth were visible. She resembled a gelatinous, translucent creature. Horrified, I screamed and shoved her away. She hit the corner of the elevator.

I wanted to flee, but the elevator was descending. I reached for the emergency button, but a man grabbed me from behind, his arms hairy and strong like a gorilla's. I struggled to break free. A third figure stood in front of me, gesturing with deformed hands that resembled boar hooves. His face, grotesque and twisted, looked like a melted wax figure, frozen in a grimace of pain. He kept howling, and just as I managed to break free from the beast-like man, the elevator doors opened, and I darted out.

The lobby of the building's reception looked like a Halloween costume party gone wrong. The atmosphere was eerie, as though the place had been scorched by fire. The elegance and vibrant colors of the once-luxurious apartment tower had been replaced by dull, blackened, moldy tones. The most unsettling part was the people—they looked like zombies, staring at me with hellish eyes and expressions of pity. My throat went dry, and I felt frozen, my legs as heavy as concrete.

I heard muffled voices until one became clear: "Are you all right, young lady?" I turned around and saw a face that looked like a child's crayon drawing in shades of red. Adrenaline surged through me, propelling me to flee from that nightmare. I ran toward the main exit, desperate for escape. Outside, reality hit me with brutal force.

The sky, once blue, had turned a blood-red hue. Towers and buildings stood matte black, their glass reflecting an amber light. The air was scorching, suffocating. It stank of burning fuel and charred meat, so intense it made me cough. What I thought were snowflakes began to fall, but when I touched them, I realized they were ash. Like inside the tower, the streets were crowded with deformed men and women, wearing old, tattered clothes.

I couldn't comprehend what was happening. I moved, directionless, through the eerie landscape. The cars appeared ravaged by the elements. Confusion overwhelmed me. *"What had happened?"* The first explanation that came to mind was a large-scale terrorist attack—perhaps the Chinese or Russians had launched nuclear bombs against the U.S., which would explain the blackened landscape and the deformities of the people. Or, *"Had the solar eclipse triggered a cataclysm?"* But if that were true, *"Why was I unharmed?"* The *barrosanctum* came to mind, and I wondered if it had protected me from the radiation or some other catastrophic effect of what seemed like a nuclear holocaust.

My thoughts were interrupted when I heard what sounded like Dante's voice calling me from afar. Hope surged through me, only to be crushed when I turned and saw the infernal being who had attacked me. He stood at the building's entrance, dressed like a beggar, rasping, "It's me, it's me," as he advanced like a charging bull. Panic took over, and I ran, screaming for help. Relief washed over me when I saw a dusty police car parked at the corner. I waved frantically as I rushed toward it.

Two officers were inside. I banged on the driver's window, and the officer stepped out. But he wasn't human. His face was a mass of blood, alive with grotesque movement, emitting incoherent sounds from a gaping mouth. My chest tightened, and my breath came in short gasps. The second officer approached, his face even more horrifying—a mass of fur and flesh, like the remains of a roadkill. One of them placed his hands on my shoulders while the other watched. In that moment, all sound vanished, replaced by a deafening ring in my ears. I felt dizzy, like I was floating. Before I knew it, the deformed rapist stood before me, arms outstretched as he lunged at me.

I awoke from a deep sleep, fighting the grogginess and confusion that clung to me. My eyelids felt heavy, my senses dulled. My dry mouth and trapped voice signaled that something was wrong. Slowly, I realized I was in a hospital; an IV needle pricked my left arm, and the medical monitors flickered in the dim room. Cold air enveloped me.

I struggled to sit up, trying to clear the fog from my mind. I clung to the hope that it was all just a nightmare. I reached for the intercom, but my movements were sluggish. Glancing toward the window, I could barely discern the night outside. The door creaked open, and a dark figure stepped in. The nurse, who reminded me of a widow at a funeral, approached my bed. My nerves tightened as she spoke, but her words were incomprehensible.

I wanted to believe this was a side effect of the narcotics they'd administered, so I asked for water and a blanket. Her reply, however, was distorted. She moved to the IV stand on the right side of the bed, checking it carefully. When she turned on the light, the nightmare returned.

Her face was gaunt, pale, and lifeless. Hollow eyes stared back at me. I screamed, and soon other nurses, equally terrifying, appeared, joined by a grotesque male figure resembling an enraged orangutan. They closed in around my bed. I tried to get up, but they pinned me down. Before I knew it, I was sinking into the bed, drifting into a blissful slumber that brought a fleeting sense of peace.

When I awoke, I was submerged in the *barrosanctum*, inside my oval bathtub of travertine and marble. The thick mixture completely enveloped my body, producing a pleasant sensation, though not as intense as the first time. I looked at my hands, my arms, and touched my face. For a moment, I thought it had all been a dream. But something was off—I wasn't in my apartment. I was in an open area I immediately recognized.

I was back in *Akeldama*. In the distance, I saw the Monastery of Saint Onuphrius, perched on the southern slope of the Hinnom Valley, along with the ruins of ancient walls and structures.

The bathtub was nestled among dense trees. Dark clouds crowded the sky, and a gentle breeze rustled the leaves. There was no one else around; it was as if the world had vanished, leaving me alone in that place.

The air was serene, filled with peace, a comfort after the hell I had just endured. I thought I heard voices calling my name. One voice, in particular, was so familiar it made my heart race.

In the distance, I spotted a woman sitting among the stones on a small hill. As I approached, I knew who she was: my mother. I stood up from the tub and walked toward her, unbothered by my nakedness; the clay served as my clothing. "Mom? Is that you?" I asked, my voice trembling. She smiled, and my tears began to flow.

I ran to her, embracing her tightly, unable to contain my emotions. She wept too. Gently, she took my face in her hands and spoke words that pierced my soul like a blade, making everything painfully clear.

"Forgive me for what I did to you, my child," she whispered, her eyes filled with tears. And then, she vanished, like sand swept away by the wind. I remained there, crying and calling out for her, until another voice jolted me from my sorrow. I searched for its source and saw a man sitting under a tree.

He smiled at me. He was only a few meters away. I approached cautiously. Though I couldn't see his face clearly, I knew it wasn't deformed; it was the face of a bearded man, which reassured me. His long black hair fluttered across his face like a veil. His gaze was sorrowful, yet piercing. His robes were strange and unfamiliar.

"Who are you?" I asked.

He smiled again, and with his right hand, he scooped up a handful of reddish earth, letting it slip through his fingers like tiny waterfalls. As he did so, he locked eyes with me and said something that I would never forget, something that clarified everything.

"The lands of Akeldama have granted you youth and beauty until your final breath. In your world, no woman is more beautiful than you. But there are costs to be paid. The lands of the potter's field demand it. The currency accepted here is betrayal and the thirst for revenge. More than anyone, you know that nothing is gained without sacrifice. You gained what you desired most in exchange for losing your ability to see the intrinsic beauty around you. Now, you see only your own. Is that a fair price?"

"I don't want it anymore! Is there a way to undo what I've done?" I asked, desperate.

The man let out a mocking laugh as he dissolved into reddish dust, merging with the bloodstained earth. *"Not with profane rituals,*" was his final reply.

A heavy rain began to fall, dissolving my clay garments. It looked like blood. I stood there, naked—not just in body, but in soul. I had never felt like this before. I ran, desperate for shelter.

I found a cluster of small hills with cave entrances, but just as I was about to enter, what I saw emerging from them made me slip and fall backward. A horde of dark, shapeless figures surged forth, their lustful gazes the only discernible feature. I scrambled to my feet, instinctively covering my breasts, now feeling ashamed, and tried to flee. Soon, I was surrounded by a crowd of depraved men who violently threw themselves at me.

When I opened my eyes again, I was back in the bed of the dark room in the *Sanatorium of Shadows*. I was alone, but not for long, as the pale, dark nurse soon entered. She muttered some words I could barely understand; something about the doctor's arrival and staying calm. I did my best to suppress any reaction, hoping to avoid another dose of tranquilizers. If I wanted to get out of there, I needed to act carefully. Shortly after, what I assumed was the doctor arrived.

He was monstrous, nearly two meters tall, with a face resembling a toad's, his skin grotesque and revolting. Guttural groans escaped his throat as he approached. I clenched my jaw, but I couldn't stop myself from screaming when he placed his disgusting hand on my chest, as if to listen with a stethoscope. Just then, another nurse entered, preparing to administer more tranquilizers, but she was interrupted by a man who appeared at the door.

This is how I met Gael. You remember I mentioned him earlier, don't you? He was the therapist assigned to my case. The first time I saw him, his physical appearance horrified me, but something in his voice calmed me. Perhaps it was because he was the first person I could fully understood, even though at times, it felt like he was speaking in a strange dialect.

Gael offered me genuine help, trying to explain what they believed was happening to me. Their diagnosis suggested I had suffered a severe emotional crisis that led to a psychotic break, characterized by hallucinations and delusions.

Of course, their diagnosis was completely wrong because, by then, I knew what was truly happening. I was purging the curse of *Akeldama*, and I wasn't sure I could survive that infernal prison.

Things took a turn for the worse when the man impersonating my beloved Dante came to visit me. No matter how much they explained or how many doses of reality they tried to inject, to me, that imposter was an abhorrent rapist, and everything about him repulsed me. Love had turned to hatred. The crisis I experienced during his visit was so intense that they sent me back to the *happy hour* of tranquilizers.

What a terrible irony, that the man for whom I had given myself to the curse of *Akeldama*, to keep his eternal favor, now caused me nothing but repulsive disgust. I never saw him again.

I stayed a few more days under observation in that hospital—which seemed to come straight out of a horror film—before being transferred to my current prison. They didn't consider it safe to discharge me yet. Despite my attempts to conceal it, they noticed my fragile emotional state, which, more than anything, was due to the terrible reality I would have to live with for the rest of my life.

From that moment on, my eyes could only perceive the most hideous aspects of this new world. I had lost the ability to see beauty. My spiritual blindness led me to a decision that became my life sentence, but I didn't care; I thought it would allow me to escape that world of visual corruption.

During my walks through the halls of the *Sanatorium of Shadows*—yes, that's the name I gave it—the doctors, including Gael, insisted I do so, supposedly to gradually restore my ability to socialize. I took advantage of a momentary lapse in the nurse's attention and managed to steal a key from the medical supply room. This key was my release from that world. I fought an internal battle, trying to summon the courage to follow through. I couldn't find the right moment or the strength to act; it was an unexpected visit that pushed me to make my decision.

Someone who identified himself as my father appeared before me. I won't describe his physical appearance because the memory is too bitter to relive. I pretended in his presence, making it seem like I was on the road to recovery, but the moment I was left alone, I broke down in tears. The situation had become unbearable, so I took the key I had hidden under my pillow—actually, a pair of sharp surgical scissors.

Without hesitation, I gathered momentum with my left hand and drove one of the sharp tips into my left eye, stifling my scream of pain. There was no turning back. Taking advantage of the adrenaline, I switched the scissors to my right hand and repeated the act on the other eye.

The sharp, stabbing pain radiated from my eyes to my brain, flooding my mind with overwhelming despair. Blood poured from my sockets, mixing with my final tears, veiling my vision with agony. Then, I plunged into an abyss of indescribable torment.

I screamed, tearing at my throat, feeling as though I were drowning in a liquid that seeped into my nostrils and mouth. And then, I lost consciousness.

That's how I ended up in the *prison* I mentioned at the beginning of this story. It's a prison in the figurative sense, one I entered willingly. Now I understand it was not only selfish but foolish.

Looking back, I realize that my blindness was the true curse of *Akeldama*. I could have learned to see things differently. The bearded man in the potter's field had told me so when I asked if there was a way to reverse my fate. But like an addict, I turned again to profane rituals, performed in the most sacred temple.

What happened to me? Thanks to Gael's intervention, I was saved from being committed to an asylum where, after what I did, I already had a permanent reservation. He poured his energy into helping me adjust to my new reality and recover from my self-inflicted injury. I spent nearly a month in the hospital before being discharged and returning to my apartment, which, it seems, retained its beauty. It's the only place where I still feel like I belong. That's why I told you it's a cell with all the comforts, where I can receive visitors.

I need to finish dictating this to my computer because Gael will be here soon to help me with a few things I requested.

I have a curious feeling after sharing all this. A fleeting but intense desire for Gael. Do you remember how I mentioned his facial sores and blisters are healing?

I'll leave you with this: Yes, I am the most beautiful woman among the hideous. I am the *Empress of Clay* in the empire of the grotesque.

FORNEUS VUAL

Detective Robert Ortega of the Los Angeles Police Department received a call from Commander Yosef Gabbai of the Jerusalem Police. It was 10:35 a.m. local time in Los Angeles; 8:35 p.m. in the ancient city. The news was urgent: they had found the suspect. Ortega's expression turned stony when he was informed of the circumstances of the discovery—the suspect was dead. Hanging. Apparent suicide. He was found near a monastery in an ancient cemetery in the old city, dangling from a tree. Ortega demanded every detail. Preliminary forensic tests indicated the death occurred around 2:10 p.m. on the same day, April 8, 2024.

The body bore bruises on the face, neck, arms, and back. Some appeared self-inflicted, while others were the result of blunt force trauma. Despite the injuries, the crime scene suggested suicide—an unsettling conclusion.

The official autopsy report would be ready in a few days, but bureaucratic delays loomed over the repatriation process. Although the crime occurred in Los Angeles, the suspect was Norwegian, and he died in Jerusalem. Local authorities needed to determine jurisdiction before anything could proceed. Only after that could the family claim the body—assuming the conflict in Israel didn't spiral out of control—and by then, Los Angeles might just receive it perfectly preserved, like a mummy.

What disturbed Ortega wasn't the logistical nightmare but the contents of the deceased's phone, left on a pile of rocks nearby. Unlocked. A video addressed to the authorities. A confession. Frustration darkened Ortega's face as he pursed his lips and furrowed his brow. His eyes, small and sharp, gleamed as he ran a hand absentmindedly through his thinning hair. He demanded Commander Gabbai send the video immediately, but Gabbai refused, citing local police protocols. Since the death occurred in Jerusalem, the investigation fell under their jurisdiction. Higher authorities would make the final decision, but it could take days.

With over thirty years of experience, Ortega was used to such hurdles. A few veiled threats—mentioning "obstruction of justice" and "U.S. Embassy intervention"—were enough to make Gabbai relent. The video was sent over.

After decades of solving complex cases, Ortega had grown weary of puzzles with no clear solution, and this case was one of those maddening enigmas. Though only two weeks had passed since the murder, it felt like years. A brutal murder had been committed, with no apparent motive or connection between the victim and the perpetrator—save for one tenuous link. Now, with the prime suspect dead, things were even more complicated.

Ortega feared this case might land in the cold case files, but the video promised to unravel the mystery. This discovery could not only reveal the truth but also save months or even years of chasing elusive evidence down a claustrophobic tunnel of dead ends. That's why Ortega nearly exploded when Gabbai initially refused to share the video.

Both Ortega and the Los Angeles Police Department struggled to understand why a Norwegian man had committed such a heinous murder in Los Angeles, only to flee to Jerusalem, where he was later found hanged, showing signs of a beating. None of it made sense. The only connection between the two events was that both the victim and the suspect were involved in music—the former a collector, the latter a musician.

When the police first arrived at the crime scene, robbery seemed the most logical motive. The victim, Mick Stephenson, was a well-known music collector with possessions worth hundreds of thousands of dollars. But to their surprise, nothing had been stolen. Despite the wealth of valuable items, the killer hadn't taken a thing.

The second disturbing element was the gruesome manner of Stephenson's death, which occurred in the early hours of March 30, 2024, at his luxurious home. The scene was nightmarish, even for the seasoned forensic team. The killer had performed the *blood eagle*— a process of ritualized torture and execution allegedly carried out during the Viking Age. Stephenson's body was found hanging from a wall in the shape of a human *X*, his arms stretched and tied to an interior balcony. His back had been sliced open, the ribs severed from the spine, and his lungs pulled out, creating a grotesque semblance of wings.

This method of execution was meant to inflict slow, excruciating pain and was historically reserved for the most hated enemies. It sent a message of terror. Yet, no connection existed between the victim and perpetrator. Who was this horrifying message for? Was it an act of revenge? Music seemed to be the only thread linking the events, but as the investigation progressed, the paths diverged. On the side of the alleged killer, information gathered by the Los Angeles Police Department revealed a criminal record in Norway.

Einar Iversen, born in 1974 in Stavanger, Norway's oil capital, had been imprisoned multiple times. He faced charges of attempted kidnapping, assault, and involvement in the notorious wave of church burnings that swept across various Norwegian cities in 1992, carried out by bands associated with the *True Norwegian Black Metal* movement.

This extreme subgenre of heavy metal was notorious for its violence, Satanism, and vocal opposition to Christianity. *True Norwegian Black Metal* featured dissonant chords, chaotic rhythms, and lyrics that evoked terrifying atmospheres steeped in Norse mythology, Satanism, and paganism. In some cases, the movement radicalized further, incorporating themes of white supremacy and Nazi ideology.

Forneus Vual was the name of the band Einar Iversen founded under the pseudonym "Torn Skinlord". He played bass and served as the lead vocalist. His bandmates included Njord "Bone Ghoul" Thorsen on guitar and Haldor "Lurid Aorta" Helland on drums. They formed the band in the early 1990s, deeply influenced by and contributing to the movement started by Øystein Aarseth, known as Euronymous, the legendary musician and founder of the band Mayhem. Euronymous was brutally murdered in 1993 by another member of Mayhem, Varg Vikernes, also a legend in the genre.

During those years, Euronymous founded a secretive group in Oslo known as the *Black Metal Inner Circle*. Comprised of individuals from various bands, the group often met in the basement of *Helvete*, a record store owned by Euronymous. This inner circle was more than a music collective, it was a cult of militant Satanists whose mission extended beyond the music itself. Their goal was to protest against Christianity, which they believed had suppressed Scandinavia's pagan roots. Many referred to them as satanic terrorists, claiming they were responsible for burning over fifty churches across Norway, allegedly led by Varg Vikernes and Einar Iversen.

Though *Forneus Vual* never recorded a full studio album, the band achieved cult status through unfinished song recordings and live performances on grim, darkened stages. Detective Ortega was struck when he watched videos of the band. He was particularly shocked by their physical appearance: they resembled blood-soaked Viking warriors after a battle, their faces painted like corpses "corpse paint"— a trademark of black metal.

In one video, Torn Skinlord, clad in a black robe, appeared to perform a ritualistic goat sacrifice on stage. The unsettling scene reminded Ortega of 1990s crime footage, with its grainy eight-millimeter quality, adding an eerie, vertiginous element.

In the band's only official photograph, the three members were displayed inside wooden coffins in a dark, old-west-style setting. Despite the poor audio quality and low production value of their music, this roughness was celebrated within the black metal community. Higher production quality, they believed, would have betrayed the genre's raw, cold aesthetic.

The band's fame within the *Black Metal Inner Circle* grew after rumors surfaced about a supposed demo recording intended to become their first album. This unreleased recording attained mythical status. Urban legends claimed that only those considered *Trve*—a term used to describe the true followers of *True Norwegian Black Metal*—would have the privilege of not only hearing the album but understanding it.

In one of Torn Skinlord's few surviving interviews, he declared that the recording would serve as their Bible, with the intention of founding a new religion. The band thus seemed determined to keep their music inaccessible to the general public.

From that point, *Forneus Vual* began to radicalize, committing acts of vandalism for which they became infamous. One such incident involved the brutal beating of four teenagers in a fast-food restaurant in Oslo during the early autumn of 1992. The teenagers had just attended a Metallica concert and were eating burgers when Torn Skinlord, Bone

Ghoul, and Lurid Aorta, along with four other members of the *inner circle*, entered the restaurant.

Witnesses reported that Bone Ghoul began mocking the teenagers for wearing Metallica shirts, and labeling them as "posers", accusing the band of selling out and betraying the true essence of heavy metal. When the teenagers responded, Lurid Aorta spat at one of them, escalating the confrontation. Torn Skinlord grabbed a chair and smashed it into the face of one of the Metallica fans, unleashing chaos.

The outnumbered teenagers were beaten severely by the seven attackers, with the violence only ending when the sound of approaching police sirens could be heard. Two of the young men suffered skull fractures, and one slipped into a coma for over a month.

Another chilling incident connected to the band made headlines when a fan, eager to join the *inner circle*, was subjected to an extreme initiation. The fan, Bjørn Larsen, was told that to truly understand black metal, he would have to face death. However, when Bjørn began to sense the sinister undertones behind Torn Skinlord's intentions and attempted to back out, it was too late. The band kidnapped him, bound him, and threw him into the trunk of Lurid Aorta's car. They drove him to a forest outside Oslo, dug a grave, and buried him alive. As Bjørn begged for his life, the band mocked him with chants.

"Welcome to the inner circle," Torn Skinlord sneered, before the three members left the scene, laughing maniacally.

By sheer luck, Bjørn managed to escape the shallow grave, saving his life. When the band was accused of the kidnapping, they tried to dismiss it as a *practical joke*. This was just one example of the twisted competition among black metal bands, each striving to prove their loyalty to the *inner circle* through ever more extreme acts of violence, all vying to become the *lords of chaos*. This competition not only included acts of terrorism, such as church burnings, but also murders carried out by members of other bands.

The dissolution of the Black Metal Inner Circle cult followed directly from Euronymous's murder in August 1993 and a string of criminal activities that sent several members to prison. In this chaotic aftermath, *Forneus Vual's* story took an even darker turn. Obsessed with their art, the band members declared that only a chosen few would be granted the privilege of hearing their new music. They claimed they were on the verge of becoming the undisputed lords of the genre and warned of dire consequences for anyone who betrayed the band, cursing them with a *doomed* fate.

These ominous declarations became a tragic self-fulfilling prophecy when Bone Ghoul and Lurid Aorta died under violent and mysterious circumstances in early December 1993. Bone Ghoul leapt from the top of a building in Oslo, while Lurid Aorta died in a horrific car crash outside the city while fleeing a police chase. He reportedly claimed demons were chasing him. His body was unrecognizable after the crash.

Whistleblowers came forward following the deaths of the two musicians. In one case, Lilja Olsen, a twenty-one-year-old woman from Bergen, told police that Lurid Aorta had raped her on the altar of an old church, which he set on fire afterward. The crime took place in 1991. Lilja had remained silent, fearing severe consequences for herself and her family, as Lurid Aorta had threatened her with violence if she reported the assault.

In another case, an anonymous source revealed that Kumar Sharma, originally from India, had been murdered by Bone Ghoul in November 1991. Rumors circulated that the killing was racially motivated, but the true motive died with the musician. Kumar's body was found buried in a clandestine grave on an abandoned farm the band used for rehearsals.

Despite the band being linked to the disappearance of seven people, no direct evidence ever connected them to these crimes.

Torn Skinlord's behavior grew increasingly erratic after these events. Many claimed he had descended into madness.

This was used as part of his defense when, in late 1994, he was arrested and sentenced to 36 months in prison for assault and kidnapping.

After his release, Torn Skinlord dedicated himself to erasing all traces of the band. He destroyed band memorabilia, publicity materials, and musical recordings. Eventually, he vanished, and even his family never heard from him again. Rumor had it that he retreated to a cabin on the outskirts of the small winter town of Lillehammer, living as a recluse.

As Detective Ortega reviewed the investigation data, he examined an old photograph of Einar Iversen taken by the Oslo police. It showed a young Einar without makeup, his long, straight blonde hair falling to his shoulders. His finely featured face appeared calm but expressionless. It was hard to believe such a face concealed a criminal of his magnitude. Only his lost, penetrating gaze hinted at a deep-seated psychopathy.

Ortega studied the footage from the security cameras at Mick Stephenson's house. The video showed a tall man, approximately six-foot-three, slightly hunched, thin, with long hair, a bushy beard, and a backpack. He entered through the back of the residence at 3:25 a.m. on March 30, 2024. Nearly two hours later, Einar walked out the front door, appearing as if nothing had happened. He didn't even bother to take the tools used in the grisly murder, indicating that covering his tracks was the least of his concerns.

According to records from the investigation, just minutes after leaving the house, Einar took an Uber to LAX, where he boarded a flight to Jerusalem. There, his trail vanished until his body was found at the legendary archaeological site of *Akeldama.*

For Ortega, this case was like trying to decipher an abstract expressionist painting. The logic behind Einar's actions was elusive. Why had Einar come out of hiding to commit a murder halfway across the world, only to flee to a country embroiled in violent conflict?

Mick Stephenson collected music-related items: special edition vinyl records, CDs, various types of cassettes, band memorabilia, guitars, and other musical instruments that once belonged to famous musicians. A report by a music expert, requested as part of the investigation, confirmed that his taste had nothing to do with the black metal genre. For these reasons, Ortega believed the video might hold the key to understanding a case riddled with bizarre inconsistencies.

The digital video file had a runtime of fifty-seven minutes and thirteen seconds. Detective Ortega downloaded it to his desktop computer and instructed his secretary not to interrupt him. Two of his closest colleagues, Officer Steve Wilkinson and Detective Lorna Baez, stayed with him.

The video was recorded in selfie mode and in vertical orientation. Initially, the image was shaky and out of focus as Einar adjusted himself in what appeared to be a grim setting. In the distance, a faint light illuminated the stone frame of what seemed like the entrance to an ancient structure. The lighting was dim, coming from the fading daylight filtering through the exterior and a flickering flame casting fleeting strokes of light, making objects appear and disappear in a constant play of shadows. This eerie ambiance intensified the investigators' emotions when Einar finally appeared on screen. He was dressed in dark clothing.

The low lighting accentuated his haunting appearance. His gaunt, sorrowful face filled the screen. Disheveled hair curled over part of his forehead and cheek. He ran his left hand over his unkempt beard, trying to smooth it down. His breathing was labored, with intermittent gasps. His gaze wasn't that of a madman but of someone deeply disturbed.

He cleared his throat before speaking in a grave, faltering voice. He spoke fluent English but with a strong accent. His words were sharp, devoid of emotion, except in certain parts where emotion seemed unavoidable. Detective Ortega's first impression upon seeing Einar's face was that they were about to hear a fanciful, delirious confession from an unstable individual. That assumption was quickly dispelled. There was something in Einar's narrative that made Ortega realize that no matter how much experience one has, human behavior remains an enigma.

"Why did I kill Mick Stephenson?" His blunt, direct opening line reverberated in the room.

"That's what you're all dying to know, but as you'll see, that's secondary. To whoever is watching this—and I hope it's fallen into the right hands—understand that this is not a confession of a crime because that pig deserved it. He was warned. I don't regret it. What I did was necessary to prevent a greater evil." He paused, frowning and pressing his lips together.

"This is a testimony I must leave for the world, so they don't make the same mistakes we did. So they don't let arrogance consume them in their pursuit of fame, which will ultimately destroy them. We made a grave mistake by disturbing things that should never have been disturbed, and as a result, we betrayed ourselves. I can't blame anyone else; we were the architects of our own ruin," he said, showing for the first time a fleeting expression of sadness.

"Greedy, malicious people tried to unleash forces they

could never understand. That's why that bastard paid the ultimate price. The supreme god passed judgment, and I was the executioner. To understand what I'm talking about, I must first tell you the backstory." He paused again, looking upward. Occasionally, the image went out of focus.

"My name is Einar Iversen. Everyone knows me as *Torn Skinlord*. I am the founder, bassist, and vocalist of the band *Forneus Vual*. I've never been good at expressing myself, and I hate talking too much. This will be the first and last time I do it. I've always preferred talking to myself, to my higher self. I am my own god and demon. We were part of a powerful, true movement that sought personal realization, liberation, the discovery of the inner self, of our own god, the one Christianity tried to suppress, enslaving humanity. That cursed ideology shackled my country for centuries, subjugated it, and stripped us of our free will. Our goal was to destroy that enemy. Yes, I took part in burning many temples of the one true false god." He paused, his face revealing no remorse.

"We are accused of being Satanists. They have no idea what they're talking about. Satan is our lord, but Christians gave him that name. They don't understand that Satan is the voice within you, the natural order that gives you freedom, the will to become superhuman. The corrupt never understood this, and they never will."

"Unfortunately, our movement became corrupted and infiltrated. We were tainted by the enemy within, and in that sense, we became *Christianized*. Many didn't grasp the true message, and neither did we at the time. Everything around us became a sinister competition—a farce. We fell into excess and into our own temptations. Like Icarus, we flew too close to the sun, and that was our downfall. I was the only one who understood it. Humanity never will. It's too late now." He massaged his temples as a faint whisper of wind could be heard in the background.

"Understand, this video's purpose is not to justify past actions. I did what I did, whether it was right or wrong. I can't speak for what Bone Ghoul and Lurid Aorta did, nor can I be responsible for their actions. They followed their own inner voices—free will. What I need to explain is the reason for their destruction. I saved myself because of the pact I made. Ironically, prison became part of my salvation. The beast lay dormant until that son of a bitch appeared—a damned infiltrator from the system," he said, his voice rising, his face reflecting anger. The microphone picked up his breathing, like that of a raging beast.

"I think I'm spinning in circles here, skirting around the core issue... It all started in September 1993 when we decided to focus on finishing the songs for what would become our debut album. We secluded ourselves in a cabin owned by Haldor's family (Lurid Aorta), deep in the woods of Nordmarka, a forested area north of Oslo. That forest held a special meaning for us; it was where we could connect with the forces of the universe. We wanted our music to be sacred. Our aim wasn't just to revive the *True Norwegian Black Metal* movement, but to ignite a real revolution. Our album was meant to be the beacon that would guide the armies of the *True* toward the destruction of Christianity. The lyrics were perfect. They spoke of forgotten pagan gods and warriors, buried in time. We called upon them to rise from their graves, to fight and destroy the unbelievers. The apocalypse that would bring about rebirth. Our music would serve as the compass for humanity's new revolution. Only a select few would be invited to join us. The unfaithful would pay the price."

"But we faced a major challenge: such a pure work couldn't be recorded just anywhere. No recording studio was worthy. It had to be recorded on enemy soil, on profane ground. That would be our first stronghold of conquest," he said, his face lit with self-satisfaction.

"We decided to record our demo at the old *Livetstre* church, located in the picturesque town of Hamar, southeastern Norway. The plan was to destroy that place of worship to the false god once the recording was done. However, a better option presented itself. It was the perfect location. I knew its history well, but until then, it hadn't crossed my mind as a possibility. An *epiphany*, as idolaters might call it. A place infested with betrayal and curses: *Akeldama*, the field of blood, purchased with the thirty pieces of silver the chief priests paid to Judas Iscariot to betray Christ. When the coward repented, he returned the blood money to the priests. Rather than return it to the temple, they bought land outside Jerusalem—a so-called cemetery for foreigners. In truth, it was used for *darker purposes*, not worth mentioning here. The important thing is, it was the *chosen place*. Our songs would be recorded on that field of blood—the perfect spot. We could barely contain our excitement."

"We set the recording date for October 31st, 1993—Samhain, when the veil between the living and the dead is at its thinnest. We kept everything secret. A week before, we traveled to Jerusalem to finalize the details. We brought only our instruments and a portable cassette recording console with four tracks—a *Tascam Porta One*. It was enough to record the guitars, bass, and drums with a single microphone. We figured we'd rent a power generator once we got there. That's all we needed. We spent a couple of days exploring *Akeldama* to find the perfect spot. If I had the time, I'd tell you about the wild times we had in that ancient city," he said with a sardonic smile, which under the flickering light gave him a dark, sinister aspect.

"At one point, we considered recording at the Monastery of St. Onuphrius, located in the potter's field on the southern slope of the Valley of Hinnom. But we rejected it—the place was constantly under surveillance. I must admit, when we set foot on that soil, we felt an indescribable emotion, standing in what ancient Judaism called Gehenna—the valley of hell, the entrance to the afterlife's world of punishment. We stayed there to meditate, and during that time, we found inspiration to compose an additional song."

"We also chose the name for our demo: *Drowning Into the Open Veins of Akeldama*," he said with pride, as if a father were boasting of his child's achievements. At this point, the video began to glitch slightly. Detective Ortega checked his computer but soon realized it was an issue with the original recording. The video continued playing.

"Recording outdoors wasn't an option. The external environment would have severely compromised the sound. We knew that if *Akeldama* had one thing in abundance, it was caves, secret passages, crypts, and catacombs. Those were the ideal places, offering the acoustics we needed. We started asking the locals in the old city if anyone could help us. A nervous teenage boy, looking like a frightened squirrel, led us to a man who prided himself on being an expert in all things related to *Akeldama*—a scholar of sorts, known to everyone as Ezra."

"When we arrived at his house, it felt like stepping into an ancient *skáli* or the hut of a *seiðr*—the equivalent of a wizard or soothsayer in Old Norse culture. The place was filled with the thick scent of incense. Ezra was attending to two men, whom he referred to as if they were characters from the Middle Ages: *Ballestero* and *Castellano*. I found the detail odd; perhaps it was because the men were speaking in Spanish," he paused, making a dismissive gesture, as if it wasn't worth elaborating on.

"When Ezra saw us, he scrutinized us with an intense gaze. After some ceremonial gestures, he asked us to sit around a circular table. I didn't waste time and, without going into too much detail, told him our goal: to record our songs in a place with sacred echoes. To my surprise, the man immediately understood the mystical intentions we wanted to infuse into our music. He launched into a long-winded lecture about the hidden powers of *Akeldama* and the importance of respecting the memory of what the place represented," Einar's expression showed frustration as he recounted this.

"I must admit, there came a point when Ezra began testing our patience with what we saw as Christian nonsense, especially when he demanded an outrageous fee to give us access and guide us through a secret Christian cemetery in *Akeldama*. A man pretending to give us moral lessons, but in reality, nothing more than a corrupt merchant of false piety. If we hadn't needed his help at that moment, we would have beaten him up. Today, I regret ignoring many of his words, which, in hindsight, were actually warnings," he lowered his gaze.

"We met Ezra at noon on October 31st, on a rocky path leading to the Valley of Hell. When he saw us with our instruments, he tried to extort more money from us. Bone Ghoul's dagger quickly changed his mind. After evading the area's security, Ezra guided us along a rugged trail beside a massive ancient fortress wall. Lurid Aorta suffered the most during the trek, as he was hauling essential parts of his drum kit on a rickety cart we had picked up at a bustling market. The small portable generator we rented also caused us a great deal of trouble. But in the end, it was worth it. Further along, hidden behind some bushes and a large dead tree, we found the entrance to the secret catacombs of *Akeldama*, where, according to legend, the first Christians, warriors, and the most notorious criminals of that era were buried. Ezra claimed that even the body of Judas Iscariot had rested there until someone stole his remains. I can't fully describe how we felt standing there. As Ezra was leaving, he said something that at first seemed like a joke, but later I wondered if it had a deeper meaning. I realized too late: *'Don't forget to close the door on your way out.'*"

"The place was spacious but dark. We illuminated it with torches and a number of black candles, which we placed in several *loculi* and *cubiculum*—old burial chambers where bodies once lay. The first few chambers we found were empty. The feeling we had was odd. Initially, we thought it was fear, but we quickly scolded ourselves, as fear was meant to be an ally for us. We couldn't afford to harbor such emotions. The atmosphere was cold, and the acoustics played tricks on our minds, as we heard faint whispers. The scent of death lingered in the air—*a delicious aroma.* We ventured further into the catacombs to find the ideal spot to set up our instruments and install the generator. Once it was running, we'd have limited time due to its finite power capacity. We would need to record all seven songs in one take. We were ready."

"At last, we found the perfect spot—a large chamber where most of the *loculi* contained bones and skulls, many forming complete skeletons. In the center, we discovered a stone sarcophagus, worn down by time. Though it was empty, we were surprised to find strange inscriptions on its sides, written in an indecipherable language. Many markings seemed violently scratched into the stone, leading us to believe they could be insults or attempts to deface the original text. Our hearts raced when we found a battered inverted cross. There was a strong possibility that this sarcophagus had once held the remains of Judas Iscariot. We had found the perfect place to record," he said, his excitement intensifying as he leaned closer to the camera, his eyes wide with a hint of madness, startling the detectives like a sudden jump scare in a suspenseful movie.

"We set everything up and connected the recording console. We arranged the bones we had collected into a pentagram on the floor and fashioned torches from the bones and old rags found with the corpses. We lit candles, casting a macabre glow across the room. It was fifteen minutes before eleven at night—the time we had chosen to begin recording, perfectly aligning with the transition from October 31st to November 1st, at the onset of Samhain."

"We decided to mix paint for our faces using clay from the *Field of Blood*. Stepping outside briefly, we performed a ritual under the moonlight. We donned black robes that sharply contrasted with our crimson-painted faces. We chanted to honor the *Æsir,* the main gods of our Viking ancestors. Returning to the catacomb, we improvised a skull as a cup and filled it with special wine mixed with a small dose of mescaline powder. With our instruments in hand, we started the generator and began recording." A sudden buzzing from the video startled the detectives, causing Baez to flinch in his chair.

"I had never experienced anything so overwhelming. Words can't capture it. We were in total communion with the great lord of darkness. The ecstasy we felt was indescribable. The music flowed with incredible power, effortlessly. I lost all sense of time. At moments, I felt as though my spirit was leaving my body—I became one with my instrument. The intensity with which Bone Ghoul played the guitar was otherworldly. Those riffs sounded like an infernal machine. The melodies were glorious. My voice surged with a supernatural force, as if a wild beast had taken hold of me. Lurid Aorta's drums pounded with such intensity that it seemed the walls might collapse under the relentless assault of the double bass, the snare, and the cymbals. Our heartbeats raced in sync with the furious rhythm of our songs. It would have been glorious—desirable even—to die right there, entombed in that cursed crypt. It would have been better," he said, bringing his hand to his face, as if to hide his expression.

"When we finished recording the seventh song and realized our first demo was complete—that we had achieved our goal of recording in *Akeldama*—we descended into madness. We began destroying our instruments like offerings in a sacrificial ritual. I took my bass and desecrated the graves, smashing skeletons until my instrument was reduced to splinters. Lurid Aorta grabbed femurs and humeri to use as drumsticks, obliterating his drumheads. Bone Ghoul, exhausted, curled up inside the stone sarcophagus for a nap, while we continued with the devastation. Eventually, we lost track of time and consciousness. The last thing I remember is waking up with a suffocating feeling, buried beneath a pile of bones. I screamed, not from fear, but because I couldn't breathe, and the sharp edges of the bones were cutting into my skin. When I finally freed myself, I found my two bandmates laughing hysterically—a pair of idiots," he laughed briefly, the sound echoing eerily through the video, sending a slight chill through Officer Wilkinson, as though he were hearing a ghost story. Ortega smiled faintly.

"When we emerged from the *Akeldama* catacomb, the sun was rising, a coincidence we took as an omen. It marked the dawn of the new masters of the *True Norwegian Black Metal* movement. We built a massive pyre out of the remains of our instruments, including the recording console, the generator, and a few bones, and set it all ablaze. We didn't give a bloody hell about the loss. It was our grand offering to our lord and master, the king of the underworld. What better way to end it than by burning the resting place of the traitor? With extreme sarcasm, we thought this would '*close the door on our way out,*' mocking Ezra's earlier words. The only thing we took with us was the recording itself. It felt surreal, holding in our hands the gospel that would ignite a new movement. We couldn't wait to see the faces of our detractors and the pseudo-followers of the genre when they heard our music. We never imagined the kind of hell we would unleash." He stopped speaking, closing his eyes as if trying to hold back tears.

"We didn't listen to the demo until we were back in Norway. You could say we had to flee from Jerusalem, as the smoke from the catacomb had drawn attention and alerted the authorities. The local newspapers blamed the incident on vandals who had desecrated the site after performing satanic rituals. Fortunately, witness descriptions were so vague that every inhabitant of the ancient city seemed like a suspect. We laughed at their confusion back then," he grimaced, shifting uncomfortably as the video flickered, his expression suddenly alert, as though he had heard something. After pausing for a moment, he continued, reassured it was just background noise.

"We organized a private ceremony to present our music to a select circle. No music critics were allowed, nor anyone who listened to genres other than black metal. We prohibited recordings, photographs, and any form of evidence. The event was strictly for the *Trves*, carefully chosen through a rigorous, almost militant process. Some attempted to sneak in, but we ensured they received the punishment they deserved."

"The event took place on November 11, 1993, in the basement of an old building in Oslo. Only seven people were invited to our musical gathering. Nothing could have prepared us for what happened that night," Einar's voice faltered here. He lowered his head and moved out of frame. His stifled sobs echoed softly. After a few moments, he returned, his eyes red and filled with anguish.

"We arranged the space like a church. The guests sat on long benches, and we positioned ourselves at an improvised altar. We assumed the role of priests, sitting like emotionless inquisitors, our faces obscured by dark crimson robes. We were the judges, silently assessing the reaction of our first parishioners. It was meant to be their initiation trial."

"We inserted the tape into a player connected to large speakers placed at the four corners of the room. The first song, 'Infernal Advocator', began. It was difficult to contain our excitement as the opening chords echoed through the room.

The song began with an acoustic intro, accompanied by bass, where I played minor-scale melodies, adding a somber tone. At an unexpected moment, a drum roll signaled the start of the assault, accompanied by dissonant riffs. The expressions on the attendees' faces were ones of shock; they exchanged bewildered glances, unsure of what they were hearing. We were exhilarated."

"As the music continued, the atmosphere grew oppressive. I felt a strange chill and a gnawing pain in my stomach, like indigestion. At first, I dismissed it. The next tracks followed: 'Purifying Impalement' and 'Executor of Annihilating Cleansing of the Soul'. But when the fourth song began— 'Drowning Into the Open Veins of Akeldama', the album's title track—my body grew impossibly heavy. I struggled to move, and breathing became labored. Looking at my bandmates, I saw they were suffering the same. Their movements were sluggish, labored. Lurid Aorta reached toward me, silently pleading for help, his eyes rolling back intermittently. Glancing at the audience, I saw them convulsing violently, as if possessed. Two were writhing on the floor. Still arrogant, I thought it was the euphoria from our music causing the effect."

"The volume escalated relentlessly. My own guttural voice stabbed into my ears, and I thought my head would split. Bone

Ghoul vomited, the foul mess clinging to his face in defiance of gravity. He couldn't move, paralyzed. The three of us were immobilized, as if bound by invisible ropes. Suddenly, the room was filled with a biting chill, and everything began to freeze. Frost descended from the ceiling as though we stood in a winter forest. The audience groaned in agony, letting out sobs and guttural wails. Panic gripped me when grotesque creatures began emerging from the walls, the main door, and even the floor. Some had torn, bloodied flesh; others had intestines spilling from gaping wounds. The stench was indescribable, overwhelming. These monstrosities looked like victims of a horrific accident or a battlefield slaughter, yet they moved with uncanny agility."

"At first, I counted five of these horrors, but soon more appeared. They swarmed the room, grotesque invaders, dancing in a circle to the rhythm of our music. Despite the cacophony of screams and moans, the music persisted. The creatures formed a violent mosh pit, tearing into one another with savage force. Blood and skin flew, the violence growing more surreal by the second. I almost convinced myself it was all a hallucination until a massive demon materialized in front of me. He towered over us, standing at least three meters tall. I remember him in excruciating detail, as if his image had been branded onto my soul with a red-hot iron." At this point, Einar abruptly stopped his tale, his face twisted in torment. The screen flickered, casting his features in an eerie light. He began coughing, the sound reverberating through the space with a hollow echo. Clearing his throat, he resumed his story.

"His skin was a pale, translucent white, so thin you could see every vein, artery, and even his internal organs. His heart beat visibly in his chest. His body was muscular, grotesquely strong. Long, matted hair fell from his skull, while a copper-colored beard partially concealed his decaying face. His mouth had been torn violently, exposing his teeth, and the cartilage of his nose dangled by threads of skin, giving it a macabre puppet-like appearance. Thick, viscous mucus dripped from his nostrils. His eyes, however, were untouched—intense, cold blue. He was clad in what first appeared to be tattered rags, but I soon recognized it as the uniform of an ancient warrior. In his left hand, as wild and savage as a raging beast, he held a massive spiked mace, from which hung strips of bloodied flesh and remnants of what I could only assume was brain matter. Never in my life had I felt such terror."

"This monstrous being crouched to my level, his face mere millimeters from mine. The foul stench that emanated from him soon invaded my lungs, burning them like fire. I coughed and vomited, the acid rising in my throat searing my esophagus. It was a harrowing sensation; my muscles refused to respond. He let out a guttural, mocking laugh that, with cruel irony, matched the rhythm of the song still playing. Lurid Aorta and Bone Ghoul stared in terror, their eyes wide as if they might burst. The giant with piercing blue eyes turned his gaze on them and spat a grotesque glob of phlegm that resembled ground meat, writhing like a mass of insects as it slid over their faces and chests. Until that moment, I had never seen such horror in their eyes. It was then that I realized how false we had always been—pretending to be malevolent to the world, while now our every fear and cowardice was laid bare."

"*Forneus, great marquis of Hell, ruler of the seas who commands twenty-nine legions of demons, make your presence known! Vual, duke of Hell, you who lead thirty-seven legions and possess the power to reveal the past, present, and future, appear at once!* —thundered the giant warrior, his voice reverberating through the place. Immediately, the pounding of drums filled the air, played with a frantic speed that assaulted our eardrums like gunfire. As in a play where the stage shifts, the frigid atmosphere morphed into something oppressive and grim, like a catacomb adorned with inquisitorial torture devices, ossuaries, and hundreds of funerary niches, illuminated solely by torchlight. In the distance, I discerned two towering anthropomorphic figures, draped in strange garments. Behind them, a horde of distorted shapes emerged. My vision clouded, and I struggled to focus. The discomfort in my body intensified, yet I retained enough mental sharpness to grasp what was unfolding. I knew what was about to occur. I will recount only part of it, for such horrors are meant to be witnessed only by those condemned to hell." A deathly silence fell. He lowered his gaze and drew a deep breath.

"By order of the giant wielding the mallet, two demons subdued one of the seven attendants. The wretched soul was paralyzed, frozen in terror by the hellish spectacle. Like a rag doll, they placed him on a St. Andrew's cross, an X-shaped wooden structure used as a torture device during the Inquisition. They flipped him upside down and shackled his wrists and ankles to the four ends of the cross. Stripping him bare, they tore away his clothes. The giant cackled maniacally, like someone possessed. My bandmates had also grasped what was happening, I could see it in their faces. Without a word, we exchanged all we needed to say. As if conjured, a massive nail gun materialized in my lap. The giant approached, laughing, and seized it in his massive hands. *Forneus Vual! Forneus Vual!* he bellowed, met with an infernal roar of approval. He approached the man on the cross, running his fingers lasciviously over the gun's barrel as if it were a phallus. He raised his arm and positioned the gun near the poor man's rectum. A long, piercing scream filled the air as the giant unleashed a volley of nails. I will not describe the horror of that scene." The camera zoomed in on Einar's face, capturing every shade of his torment.

"I knew every move the demons would make next, every word they would speak, and what terrified me most: how and when it would all end. I wasn't gifted with foresight. The truth was, we had written it. Everything happening at that moment was our songs coming to life. They unfolded perfectly, like a cinematic script, with painstaking detail and the same seething hatred we poured into our music. My heart thudded in my chest as I grasped what would happen when our seventh song played. Its name said everything. It's not worth repeating. I had to stop it, no matter what. I knew exactly how to end it."

"I summoned a superhuman effort to rise. The cacophony of demonic voices, screams, sobs, and moans of agony, mingled with our music, became a deafening, piercing roar that ripped through my ears like thousands of claws shredding my auditory canal. It left me disoriented. My legs burned as if acid had been poured over them. I have no idea where I drew the strength from, but despite the pain, I managed to get on my feet. Everything hinged on reaching the audio player to stop the tape. As I moved, I noticed the giant had sensed my intentions. He seized his massive mallet and charged at me. I forced myself to move faster, each step driving searing agony through me. Just as I neared the player, I tripped and fell on my left arm. A loud crack echoed, like a branch snapping in two. The pain didn't hit right away—not until I saw the bone jutting out from my arm and my hand hanging limply, like it was made of clay. The giant was barely a meter away. If not for a sudden rush of adrenaline, triggered by fear and the searing pain, I would never have managed to press the *stop* button and pull the tape from the player." Einar paused, visibly rattled, struggling to catch his breath. Sweat dripped from him.

"Like ash in the wind, the giant crumbled into a heap of crimson dust, as did the other demons. The entire apocalyptic scene collapsed in a suffocating cloud that darkened everything. Only a faint light flickered at the far end of the hall. Some despairing laments lingered in the air. My bandmates and I lay on the ground, struggling to rise, brushing ash from our faces. The pain was unbearable. I tore off my cloak and wrapped it around my injured arm. A final reminder of the underworld remained, as if to confirm it hadn't been a dream. That haunting image shattered what was left of our souls."

"The seven unfortunate attendants formed a circle. They were impaled. The tip of the stake that pierced through them emerged from what remained of their mouths. They were still alive. Their pitiful, babbling sobs could be interpreted as pleas for help. The harrowing scene didn't leave much of an impression on us, as in one of our songs, we had already decreed it. The impaled ones were the last to turn into crimson-colored dust. For years, we were suspected of being responsible for the disappearance of those seven people. With what I've revealed here, it's clear that we were indeed to blame" he pursed his lips, and a slight tremor could be seen in his chin.

"In that forsaken place, Lurid Aorta and Bone Ghoul lost their souls. It wasn't madness, as some claimed. Our music had embedded itself in their minds, replaying every note daily. They spent nearly a month trapped in the world we had created in our demo, *Drowning Into the Open Veins of Akeldama*. They suffered the horrors we had written without escape. Both were hunted by *Moloch*—the giant of Hell who presided over the tortures in our songs. That was his name. We sang of him—the demonic deity of sacrifice of infants, who also demands the sacrifice of those who worship him, offering up their most precious possessions in exchange for their own ruin. And I summoned him. When I learned of their deaths, I felt only relief for them. Perhaps, by now, you wonder: how did I survive? Why wasn't I pursued?"

"While still in the basement, my bandmates wandered like living corpses, their faces streaked with tears and ash, an ironic mask of grief. I writhed in agony from my broken arm, crouched in a corner. I wasn't sure if what happened next was a hallucination, but now I know it wasn't. A faint voice called my name. When I turned, a blurry figure appeared; a man with long hair, a thick beard, and a tattered robe. His words were cryptic, but I understood his message: *'You saved the world from a greater evil, which is why you will live. Do you now understand the hell you unleashed by meddling with forces beyond your comprehension? Pride sealed your fate. Keep that recording. You are now its guardian, the custodian. Do not let it fall into bloodstained hands like yours. In time, you will have to repair the damage at the place you desecrated. The music must be silenced. You will close the door...'* I knew who he was and what I had to do." He fell silent. The only sound left was the faint, erratic hiss of the recording.

"Why did I kill Mick Stephenson? As I said at the start of the video, that son of a bitch begged for it. While in prison, I received all kinds of letters from the band's fans. Sometimes, sacks full of them arrived, along with strange junk. To most, we became cult figures, fictional characters, objects of worship. We turned into a vile caricature, a mockery, something we always tried to avoid. Everyone asked about our demo: why had we never released it? When would it come out? Some even doubted its existence, while others claimed to interpret covers of the unreleased songs. Of course, I knew that wasn't possible. Only seven miserable souls had the misfortune of hearing it."

"They wrote all sorts of nonsense and absurd requests. Some sent photographs with our faces tattooed on their bodies; others claimed to communicate with the ghosts of Lurid Aorta and Bone Ghoul. There were even those who built effigies of them to invoke during supposedly black masses. And then, there were death threats from religious groups, of course. I remember one fool sending a strange poem, which turned out to be a *spell* meant to leave me catatonic, as I later discovered while studying arcane texts in prison. By then, I was fed up and ready to leave everything behind, but fate was exacting cruel revenge. I stopped reading letters, destroying anything that was sent. Yet, for some reason, one letter caught my eye. Maybe it was the return address: Los Angeles, California. I had received letters from much of Europe and Latin America, but very little from the U.S., and even less from California. A strange intuition made me open it. The sender was Mick Stephenson. Its content shook me, destroying my peace of mind. How the hell did he know?"

"Mick Stephenson, introducing himself as one of the most renowned music collectors in the U.S., claimed in his letter that he knew we had recorded a demo in Jerusalem, of which only one copy existed. He offered me five hundred thousand dollars for it. He even promised to connect me with a major U.S. record label interested in releasing and promoting the demo as a full album and creating a documentary about *Forneus Vual*. The idea: to reveal our work to the world. Can you fucking believe it?"

"At first, I was furious, which quickly turned into extreme concern. How did he get that information? Who told him? Why was he interested in a genre that wasn't, and still isn't, commercial? From that moment, the little peace I had in my imprisonment became paranoia. I went weeks without sleep. My constant companion now was nightmares of *Moloch*, the infernal giant" he placed his hand to his forehead and shook his head.

"While I remained in prison, Stephenson kept sending letters, increasing his offers. But no amount of money would make me give up that music. Especially not to an unscrupulous merchant who wanted to commercialize it on a massive scale. I had a mission and wouldn't make the same mistake twice. My final days in prison were sheer torture because, even though I had hidden the recording, I knew it wasn't safe until I had it back, especially with people willing to pay so much to get it."

"Upon my release, I knew my only option was to disappear forever. It was essential to cut all ties with fans, friends, even my family. I had to sever everything connected to *Forneus Vual* and the cult that surrounded it. I destroyed every video, recording, t-shirts and any other promotional item related to the band and threatened legal action against anyone distributing our material without my express permission. With what little money I had left, along with some borrowed from my parents, I built a secret refuge in the forests outside Lillehammer. I stored the demo in a safe there. No one could find out where I was. I didn't disclose my location. I lived as a hermit, with nature as my only companion. My only communication was through letters I deposited and picked up at the local post office. I must admit, I had never been happier."

"Mick Stephenson continued to search for me after my release. He called my parents' house several times and tried contacting old acquaintances from the black metal scene. Fortunately, our circle was tight-knit, and he ran into an impenetrable wall. Soon, he stopped trying. I never heard from him again. What a fool I was" he said, shaking his head with frustration. The image trembled as Einar briefly disappeared from view. He coughed and cleared his throat.

"Thirty years later, the nightmare returned. Why such persistence? Who was behind him? I started to believe Stephenson's presence was a test of my worthiness as the guardian of the recording. I shouldn't have kept it for so long. My cowardice in not destroying it played a big role. But I must be honest; the idea of returning to *Akeldama* terrified me. How could anyone be prepared for that?"

"It was Friday, March 22, 2024, in the morning when I came face to face with that bastard. I had gone to a small town near my cabin to buy some supplies and other things I needed. As I left the local store, someone called my name: 'Mr. Iversen!' he shouted. To this day, as I record this video, I still don't understand how he managed to recognize me. Since my release from prison, I hadn't allowed a single photo of myself."

"When I turned, I saw him rushing toward me. He was in his fifties, with graying hair and a slim build, his appearance deceptively friendly. My first impression was that he was a typical wealthy American executive, clueless about how to spend his money, chasing exotic thrills. He wore glasses, which gave him a slight resemblance to Bill Gates. Dressed in a Mötley Crüe t-shirt, jeans, and Skechers, he looked like a *poser*, simply pathetic."

"'Mr. Iversen, you're hard to find. First of all, it's a great pleasure to meet you. My name is Mick Stephenson,' he said, extending his hand with what I could tell was false politeness. At that moment, my blood began to boil. The old demons of my youth stirred within me. Though my first instinct was to punch his smug, grinning face, I decided to keep things civil. I couldn't let him provoke me. 'Look, I don't know who you are or how you found me, but I'll say this once: the answer is no! There's no offer you can make that will change my mind, so stop wasting your time, understand? The answer is no. Besides, that recording doesn't exist anymore,' I snapped, my voice sharp. 'But please, Mr. Iversen, hear me out. Come on, let me treat you to lunch at the restaurant across the street. A nice meal, a bottle of wine, and we can discuss my proposal. It's in your best interest. You could be rich overnight,' he had the audacity to say, smiling like an idiot, while placing his hand on my shoulder as if we were old friends. He dared to invade my space."

"I couldn't hold back any longer and threw a hard punch at his face, then followed with one to his stomach. He collapsed on his back. For a split second, the urge to stomp on his head flashed through my mind, crushing it like a watermelon, but I resisted. As he lay there groaning, I leaned over him. 'If you ever come near me again, it won't just be a punch. You'll get something much worse. Consider this your final warning,' I growled." Einar's face filled the screen, as if reliving the moment, his gaze dark and menacing.

"I was ready to kick him a few more times when a crowd began to gather. I had to flee, fearing someone might call the police. As I made my way back to the cabin, I kept checking over my shoulder, though the likelihood of being followed seemed slim, thanks to the secluded path and the hidden security fence I'd installed. For the next four days after that run-in, I locked myself inside the cabin. I didn't go near the door. I only glanced through the windows. I knew it was nearly impossible for anyone to find me, yet I couldn't shake the feeling of unease, and I wasn't willing to take any chances."

"On the fifth day, Wednesday, March 27, I ventured outside again. I thought Stephenson had finally gotten the message. I did my usual seven-kilometer walk along my regular path. Walking always helped me relieve stress, clear my head, and check for anything unusual. Afterward, I started chopping firewood. While doing that, I felt a blow to the head, and everything went black."

"I forced my eyes open with great effort. It was hard to focus; everything was a blur. I realized I was lying on the ground, my face buried in dirt, my beard tangled with dry leaves. I was face down. A stabbing headache hit me like a rabid dog sinking its teeth in. I tried to rise but failed at first.

For a moment, I couldn't remember where I was or what had happened. I looked up at the sky—it was getting late, and a cold breeze crept into my bones. I finally managed to stand, though I felt unsteady. I touched the spot where I'd been struck; a lump had formed, and the blood had already dried. My mind scrambled to piece things together, like a computer rebooting. "*What the hell happened?*" I muttered. The answer struck me instantly. Panic surged through me, and I stumbled toward the cabin, barely able to stay on my feet. The door was wide open. I practically crawled inside. I hadn't felt such a crushing sense of doom since the day our demo first debuted. I went straight to the safe: it was open. I collapsed onto the floor and wept uncontrollably." Einar raised a hand to his forehead, squinting. He took a deep breath.

"I struggled to regain my composure, knowing I needed to act swiftly and think clearly. I suspected who had stolen the recording, but I had to confirm it. I went to the room where my laptop was. I opened the app that controlled the security cameras I'd hidden throughout the cabin and its perimeter. I checked the video files. Sure enough, while I was out on my walk, three black Toyota Land Cruisers had pulled up at the security gate. A man in dark tactical gear stepped out and took his time figuring out how to bypass the gate. He eventually succeeded. They parked in the blind spots. The cameras didn't catch their movements afterward."

"In the footage, I appeared, chopping wood. Two men dressed in black crept up behind me, and one of them struck me on the head with what looked like a baton. They worked quickly, no question they were professionals. Four more men joined them, and together they broke down the door with a few solid hits. Shortly after, Mick Stephenson appeared. Confirmed. The bastard had ignored my warning and raided my cabin to steal the demo. I watched the whole thing unfold on the screen, helpless and furious. I began to cry again, this time in sheer rage. How could I have been so stupid, so careless? But there was no time for regrets. It was time to act, and fast."

"It was obvious Stephenson had hired professionals to steal the recording. They'd been on my trail for a while. But Stephenson? He wasn't one of them. He was just a pompous fool, some rich guy with more money than sense. His ego was enormous, and his attitude worse. He hadn't even bothered to cover his tracks, proving he was no professional. Honestly, he was an idiot for not killing me when he had the chance. It would have been easy, no one would have missed me. Maybe years would've passed before anyone found my body, if they ever did. Wild animals could have done the dirty work. But none of that mattered. Stephenson, like us, was arrogant and self-absorbed, obsessed with media attention and addicted to flaunting himself on social media. Tracking him down wasn't difficult. He practically broadcast his location in every post about his ridiculous music collection. He'd been the subject of several articles detailing the extravagant, wild parties he threw at his mansion with the heavy metal crowd" Einar let out a bitter laugh.

"It was time to act. That same day, I headed to Oslo, then straight to the airport. I bought the first available flight, though it didn't leave until the next day, which worked against me. Time wasn't on my side, but I had no choice but to wait. I couldn't let that idiot make copies of the recording. After a long flight, I arrived in Los Angeles on Friday, March 29th. I almost didn't make it through immigration because my criminal record set off alarm bells. Thankfully, after an extended interrogation, I convinced them I was visiting Mick Stephenson for an important music project. It wasn't a lie. Fortunately, they bought it when I showed them photos of him and his connection to the music industry."

"I scoped out his residence, lingering nearby to assess my options. He was so careless; he hadn't even bothered to hire security. He must've thought I was dead, either from the blow or that nature had taken care of it. What an idiot. The guy lived alone. He was divorced, and his kids lived with their mother.

Apparently, they couldn't stand his wannabe rock star lifestyle or his preference for prostitutes. Blessed social media—it told me everything."

"While waiting, I used the time to buy what I needed at a nearby hardware store. Mick Stephenson was going to pay for what he did. Since it was Friday, I worried he might throw one of his infamous parties. Thankfully, he went out instead. I considered breaking in while he was gone, but I decided it was smarter to wait. He might come back with someone, which would complicate things. He returned at 2:42 a.m. I waited at a nearby 24-hour coffee house, watching the minutes tick by. When the time came, I slipped through the service door. It was almost too easy. I went upstairs to his room, and there he was; snoring, completely unaware of the hell he could had unleashed. I decided to wake him with a hammer blow to the shin. The bastard screamed like a wounded dog. The rage burning inside me was so intense I could've unleashed the fury of a thousand Vikings on him, but I forced myself to stay focused. I had to recover the recording." Einar paused briefly, the video shaking as footsteps echoed. The screen went dark for a moment. Then his face reappeared, and he continued.

"When he saw me, the pathetic thief turned pale, like he'd seen a ghost. He trembled and begged for his life. I thought I might struggle to get him to hand over the recording, but as soon as I brandished the massive, razor-sharp machete I'd bought, Stephenson broke down, weeping like a terrified child. He led me to a large vault in a vast room, where he kept his most prized possessions. He wouldn't stop talking, babbling about his Jimi Hendrix and Eddie Van Halen memorabilia. Maybe he thought he could distract me. I wasn't in the mood, so I hit him hard in the jaw. 'Give me the recording already, you son of a bitch,' I shouted at him. Apparently, the recording meant a lot to him because he'd locked it in a small safe. Relief flooded over me when I finally held it in my hands again. I inspected it carefully to ensure it was the original. I recognized it instantly; the label bore my handwriting, along with a mark I'd etched into one corner."

"It was time to settle the score. Mick Stephenson was a despicable excuse for a human being, a worthless intruder who had already been warned. He crossed the line, and what enraged me the most was that he had no idea what he'd almost unleashed. He could have triggered the apocalypse—hell on earth—if he had distributed thousands of copies of that recording. I screamed this in his face. He just stared at me like an imbecile."

"One question gnawed at me relentlessly, stirring both confusion and fascination: How had he even discovered the recording? And what drove his obsession? He hadn't just thrown money at it, he'd orchestrated an entire operation to steal it. His initial responses were a mess of contradictions, barely making sense. Maybe it was the adrenaline, or my own fury, that clouded my perception. But before I could proceed with the ritual, I needed his full confession. Maybe I pushed too far" he said, brushing his hair back and letting out a sigh. At this point, the video's audio started to distort, and his voice broke intermittently. Detective Ortega frowned, leaning in and adjusting the audio controls with tense fingers.

"I ripped out a few of his nails and severed a couple of his finger joints. His cowardice was laid bare. He kept insisting that after learning about our band, the rumors, and the tragedies surrounding us, he became obsessed with the recording because it had become a cult object that everyone talked about. Between sobs, he swore there was nothing more to it. I didn't want to waste any more time, time was already my enemy.

"Before performing the *blood eagle* on him, I beat him savagely and crushed his testicles with a ball-peen hammer. I have to admit, while doing it, snippets of our songs started playing in my head. I wasn't myself. Looking back, I realize that my bloody actions were driven by the cursed demon *Moloch*. I knew then he was my master and that he would never leave me." His tone conveyed a sense of resignation. Suddenly, his face showed concern as a faint thud echoed in the distance. The video shook, and Einar's shadowed profile became visible, still and alert. He quickly refocused the camera on himself and continued.

"My time is running out. I think I've stretched this confession longer than I should have. So now you know why I killed Mick Stephenson. It was an execution to prevent a greater evil, as well as to avenge what he'd done. Now it's time to end this once and for all. To extinguish the cursed fire we unleashed. I should've done it sooner. My cowardice might've led to millions dying. And now here I am, in *Akeldama*, at the place where it all began. A place we defiled. I don't know how this will end, but I know what I must do. I have to face *Moloch*, who's already waiting for me at the gates of hell, to make amends and return the seven songs to where they should have stayed. I hope the world won't judge us too harshly."

Einar's stoic expression, maintained throughout most of the video, finally broke as he spoke these final words. His eyes filled with tears, and his lips quivered, revealing the face of a man tormented by regret and sorrow. He seemed like a completely different person. Before the video ended, a sob could be heard, followed by a strange, unintelligible voice in the background. The screen went black.

Detective Ortega rested his elbows on the desk, his gaze distant, his expression unreadable. In contrast, Officer Wilkinson and Detective Baez sat in stunned silence, their faces tense with disbelief. No one dared break the silence. What could they say? The quiet stretched on for over five minutes. There was too much to process, too many details to verify. But none of that mattered now; the critical pieces to close the case were already in hand. The confession was clear, and the evidence aligned with it perfectly. They could avoid a lengthy judicial process—the killer was already dead.

There was nothing left to investigate; no theft, no sign of third-party involvement. The rest of it sounded like the plot of a horror novel, or perhaps the deranged fantasies of a lunatic. It wasn't something that concerned the LAPD. But for those obsessed with the paranormal, this case would be a feast, a spectacle waiting to be dissected by investigators who thrived on the inexplicable.

"What do you think, boss? Can we close this case?" Detective Baez asked.

Ortega glanced at her from the corner of his eye, then broke into a broad smile. He nodded.

A month after Mick Stephenson's murder case had been closed, Detective Baez informed Ortega she'd found something interesting while labeling and boxing the evidence for storage: a CD copy of *Forneus Vual's* demo. Handwritten on the disc was the title: *Drowning Into the Open Veins of Akeldama*. It seemed Stephenson had made a copy after all.

"What do you think, boss? In the mood for some *black metal*, or should we just send it to storage?" Baez asked, her tone tinged with sarcasm.

Ortega took the CD in his hands and examined it closely. He frowned, locking eyes with Baez. He said nothing.

THE HACIENDA OF THE HANGED MAN

"Where are you headed, young man?" asked the old man, not in a reproachful tone, but rather with concern.

The young man, accompanied by his girlfriend, stopped in his tracks. They were in their twenties—tourists from the capital.

"We're going to the *Hacienda of the Hanged Man*," he replied with forced politeness, though they could have easily ignored him as a nosy stranger. They resumed walking, but the old man interrupted again, this time in a tone of warning. Solemn, with a furrowed brow, he said, "Haven't you heard about the curse that haunts not only the place but everyone who steps onto that cursed land?"

The young man gave a mocking smile. She, on the other hand, looked intrigued by what seemed to be a serious warning.

"With all due respect, sir, those are just legends, like the kind people around here love to tell. They enjoy making up ghost stories, blowing things out of proportion."

"I know the legend—it wasn't some supernatural phenomenon, but a vendetta between drug traffickers over stolen land. If there was any curse, it was the *bullet curse*. We just want content for our social media," he replied, with a hint of insolence.

The old man smiled, took off his worn fedora, and wiped the sweat from his brow. He gestured for them to sit at the rickety table on the porch, where he rested in the shade. It was only eleven in the morning, but the early July heat had already become oppressive, especially in this desert region.

The couple hesitated, exchanging quick glances of distrust.

"Please, listen to my story. What I have to tell you about that place might save your soul. If, after hearing it, you still decide to go, I won't stop you," he said with a shrug.

"At least I'll have done my part."

Reluctantly, they accepted. They pulled up chairs and sat down beside him.

The old man reached for a bottle of *Sotol* from a small side table and poured three glasses. *Sotol*, a regional liquor distilled from the Chihuahuan desert, well known for its earthy flavor. Before they could refuse, he insisted in a sharp tone.

"You'll need it to stomach what I'm about to tell you. It's aged—you'll like it," he said, with a friendly wink. Clearing his throat, he began.

"They aren't legends. They should be," he said, melancholically, without lifting his gaze. He took a sip of *Sotol*.

"I knew Don Indalecio Castellano, the owner of the *Hacienda of San Telmo*. I've been a sort of gatekeeper ever since, warning travelers, trying to keep them from entering cursed lands. This isn't a place for ghost hunters. It's not like sneaking into a cemetery at midnight for a scare—it's far worse. Whoever enters stains their soul with the remnants of vengeance and betrayal. There's nothing sweet about revenge. Some people take their time to plot it, but that only starts an endless cycle of damnation, which destroys what one holds most dear—just like it happened to Don Indalecio."

The young man watched him, still skeptical. She, however, seemed captivated by the old man's words. Something in his eyes told her he was telling the truth. He didn't seem like an ignorant local.

"Yes, it was a reckoning, but not under the *bullet curse*. It was under the curse of Judas Iscariot," he said, as a shadow crept into his eyes. The couple shivered. Just hearing the name gave them an unsettling feeling. The old man drank more *Sotol* and, grimacing, urged them to do the same.

162

Janos, situated in the far northwest of the state of Chihuahua, near the U.S. border, is where the *Hacienda of San Telmo* stands—a property that had always belonged to Don Indalecio's family, even before the Mexican revolution. These lands were spared from being requisitioned by Pancho Villa's army when his grandfather proved his loyalty to the general by enlisting in his *northern division*, avoiding being branded a landowner and exploiter of peasants. All this to protect his land. Such was his love for the land that he preferred to risk his life and pay the price in blood. The war left its scars, but he kept his land, which was passed down from generation to generation until it came into the hands of Don Indalecio.

It all began one Sunday in October 1999. Don Indalecio was enjoying the day with his family, children, and grandchildren—grilling meat and drinking beers. The peace was shattered when, in the distance, they saw a dust storm kicked up by a convoy of luxury Suburbans. Their arrival signaled trouble. The vehicles parked with reckless arrogance. Thirty men, uniformed and heavily armed, stepped out. In the background, as if it were martial music, the loud choruses of *Chalino Sanchez's narcocorridos* echoed. These men weren't police or military; they wore cowboy attire—boots made from exotic animal skins and dazzling gold jewelry. They were the lords of the drug trade.

Acting like the army of Genghis Khan, they began destroying the property, hurling threats and insults. They brandished high-caliber weapons, firing shots to stir chaos and demanding to be fed. Barbarians. At gunpoint, they subdued Don Indalecio's family, threatening to rape his wife and daughter. It was all a show of power, making it clear that they were now in charge.

Like a feudal lord, the head of the cartel, Septimio Garza, introduced himself. He demanded that Don Indalecio be brought before him, forced to kneel at gunpoint. The capo's demand was absolute.

"I like your land; I've had my eye on it for a while," he said with smug arrogance.

"It's strategic for my business, given how close it is to the gringos. Here's what we're going to do: in three weeks, we'll meet at the notary's office so you can transfer the deed to me, with all the rights and privileges that come with it. The price I'll pay you is more than fair: the life of your family, and on top of that, you get to keep your *dick*. How does that sound?" he asked with a cruel laugh.

"Three weeks, you bastard!"

"As you can imagine, Don Indalecio was devastated, and his family was in shock. How could he lose his legacy like that?"

"The capo wasn't bluffing, and his reputation as a man of his word was infamous."

Don Indalecio was a well-known figure, a northerner in both body and soul, deeply rooted in his land. He had friends among the high-ranking politicians in the capital. He decided to call in some favors, hoping to use his connections in a last effort to save his property. They turned their backs on him. Others brazenly showed their submission to the local cartel boss. Lawmakers and judges could not hide their complicity in the narco's dealings. Miserable corruption. As was typical, the police and bureaucrats in the nation's capital excused themselves with elaborate speeches and hollow promises.

"Don't be foolish, Don Indalecio. It's not worth risking your life over a few insignificant acres. You'll have the chance to buy better land someday," said some of the more indifferent ones. To Don Indalecio, their suggestions stung like needles under his fingernails.

Don Indalecio's hope evaporated, and he was lost. His spirit slowly crumbled. His attachment to the land was immense—it was part of his very being. His family tried to convince him it was better to resign himself to the situation. They talked about leaving the country, finding a better life. The most important thing was to stay alive. He finally agreed, though his morale was utterly shattered.

Two weeks remained until the signing of the deeds. In the early hours of Tuesday the 13th, lying in bed, tormented by insomnia, a cryptic memory suddenly resurfaced. It was something someone had told him years ago, during a visit to distant, ancient lands. Something arcane, hidden in the shadows of time. A desperate, almost mad idea to save his land. Madness, no doubt, but what did he have to lose?

At first light, he awoke with a renewed sense of purpose and spoke to his family. The decision was made—they would move to the United States. Citing concerns for their safety, he begged them to leave Janos that same week while he stayed behind to wrap up business and arrange the transfer of the Hacienda. It was something he had to do alone. He also spoke to all the Hacienda's workers, and it pained him deeply to let them go. He gave them generous severance pay for all their years of service and explained the dire situation they faced. The wisest thing, he told them, was to abandon the Hacienda, as the Narcos might not spare their lives.

Most of them offered to take up arms to defend the land. It was a noble cause. Don Indalecio thanked them from the depths of his heart, but the solution he had in mind would be far more effective.

That same week, Don Indalecio traveled to the ancient city of Jerusalem, a journey shrouded in mystery. He returned with two enormous crates. Today, I can tell you what they contained—soil from *Akeldama*, which he scattered across the entire Hacienda as if planting seeds.

He spent several days doing this. Many believed he had lost his mind, that revenge had consumed him. They say that on the last day Don Indalecio spent on his beloved land, he cried like a wounded wolf beneath the full moon, his sobs inconsolable.

When the infamous day arrived to sign over the deeds, Don Indalecio appeared at Public Notary Office No. 66. The notary, surely in league with the cartel boss, waited with the papers prepared. As Don Indalecio gripped the pen, his hand trembled. His face reflected deep sorrow, but also a strange satisfaction.

The next day, he left Janos, convinced he would return soon. Thanks to his plan, it would all feel like a terrible nightmare. He would invalidate the signed deeds, claiming they were signed under threat and violence. After all, soon there would be no one left to claim them. Yes, that's what he intended to do.

Septimio Garza took possession of the *Hacienda of San Telmo*, feeling even more powerful. Now he was the master of vast lands, the absolute ruler of the region. A lavish celebration was planned to last an entire week, filled with Sinaloan *banda* music. No expense would be spared. The capo's lieutenants, politicians, celebrities, and, of course, beautiful women to fulfill every lustful fantasy of the guests, were all invited. But neither the capo nor his criminal army had any inkling of the kind of celebration awaiting them.

The soil from *Akeldama* carried seeds, but they were seeds of betrayal and vengeance beyond imagination. They were nourished by the burning thirst for revenge of the one who had scattered them. Terrible demons—infernal beings— would appear at the drug lord's party, led by the malevolent energy of one who, in life, had been Judas Iscariot. His specter was the first thing the capo noticed during the festivities.

Septimio held a bottle of Buchanan's when, in the distance, he saw something that froze him in terror. A man was hanging from a tree, a noose around his neck. Suddenly, the figure came to life, freed itself from the rope, and walked slowly toward him. Septimio stood paralyzed. The specter pointed at him and let out a chilling, maniacal laugh.

In that instant, all hell broke loose. A spectral army of decayed Roman soldiers, along with mercenaries from the ancient valley of Hinnom, attacked the cartel members and their guests with merciless fury. Poor devils, they didn't even have time to fire their assault rifles. The celebration turned into a nightmare of terror—flames, screams, blood, and entrails scattered everywhere.

The final fate of the most powerful drug lord was horrific. An unimaginable fury consumed his flesh, leaving nothing but his bones. His screams of terror and desperation echoed for miles. The people of Janos couldn't sleep that night.

The police did not respond immediately, knowing the Hacienda now belonged to the cartel, where a bacchanal was in full swing. They had orders to turn a blind eye. What caught their attention was the reports, not of celebration, but of agonizing cries. Curiosity got the better of them, and they approached the scene. What they found horrified them.

It's said that many police officers experienced the same terror the cartel had faced. Some townspeople who ventured close ran away in fear, overtaken by a madness that gripped their souls. From that day on, no one dared approach what became known as *"The Hacienda of the Hanged Man."*

News of the events reached Don Indalecio. He felt joy knowing his plan had succeeded. The soil from *Akeldama* had done its work. His Hacienda was free. He returned to Janos to see for himself. As he set foot on his old land, he didn't witness the horrors described by the townspeople, but he felt an overwhelming sense of desolation and something far worse— an insatiable thirst for revenge and a crushing sense of guilt. It was unbearable. He felt watched. In the distance, he saw the shadow of a man hanging from a tree, who, in a somber voice, asked him, "*Do you now understand the price?*"

"That was the price of *Akeldama*, the same price Judas Iscariot paid when he realized the magnitude of his betrayal. He lost everything."

"What is *Akeldama*?" the young woman asked.

The old man smiled.

"That will be the last thing I tell you. *Akeldama* is also known as the Field of Blood. It's the land purchased by the ancient priests with the thirty pieces of silver Judas Iscariot received for betraying Jesus. After the betrayal, Judas, overcome with guilt, returned the money to the priests and hanged himself in that very field. It became a cursed place, forever associated with treachery and spilled blood. Whoever takes a handful of that soil to scatter in vengeance or betrayal will be condemned for eternity."

The old man finished his story. The young couple now had tears in their eyes. They knew his words held the truth. Now they understood the path they had to follow.

THANK YOU FOR MAKING IT THIS FAR!

It has been an honor for me to have you journey through these pages. Now, your voice is essential for this work to continue its life beyond these pages.

I invite you to leave a review and share your thoughts. Your opinion will not only help me grow as an author, but it will also guide other readers who are looking for their next great read. Leaving a review is simple and can be done on the platform where you purchased this book or on your favorite social media. Don't forget to tag me so I can read your thoughts and thank you personally.

Thank you again for joining me on this literary adventure. I eagerly await your words with anticipation and gratitude.

Jose Neptuno Martinez

www.ingramcontent.com/pod-product-compliance
Lightning Source LLC
Chambersburg PA
CBHW020127180626
46810CB00004B/1432